Falling Har...

- Nine Slightly True Short Stories -

By
JT DeBold

I dedicate these stories to those who
give their all to live their dreams.

CONTENTS

Dedication

Prologue

About the Author

Prologue

History is a perpetual realm and resource expanded continuously by the passage of time. It often brings boredom to our youth and reflection in our later years. At times, we dispute it but still honor it for the mark it makes upon our lives, good or bad. History is often fabricated in order to fill the unknown gaps between dueling facts.

Curiosity creates a need to know more about the world around us. This includes the lives of strangers. We speculate, repudiate and fabricate the details of the detrimental choices by others. We don't always have a right to know why one lives their life in turmoil but it entertains us. It's that entertainment that is the basis for this book.

Taking historical facts and blending them with a plausible dose of speculation takes the lives of nine true-to-life celebrities and brings theory to their detriment and demise. Among the characters are two friends with identical origins. One found fame and fortune while the other never got past obscurity because she gave-up her chance.

There was the actress who discovered her husband's truth only to die of mysterious circumstances. Never shall the truth be known. There were the studio leaders who contributed to the casting couch. They were brought down by a movement of people silenced by fear. Another scandalous character was an A-list actress who derailed her career by marrying her former step-son after love had failed her.

There was the actor whose sex addiction subsidized his career as he struggled to remain a viable star. The circumstances of his demise remain a mystery to this day. Other stories include the singer who fell hard from drug addiction; the comedian whose life was no laughing matter and the dancer whose life was seemingly cursed.

These nine short stories are fictional accounts of the tragic lives of past and present Hollywood characters. They bring to the reader the mystery of fact versus fiction. Names are fictitious but what else is not? Historical gaps are pervaded by the speculation surrounding those who would find themselves falling hard in Hollywood.

Chapter One

Anything for a Friend

Smoke permeated the crowded confines of a small, back lot bar like it was a decoration equal to that of the shabby chic knickknacks on the walls. Blaring, toe-tapping sounds of 1930s music were being pounded out at the corner piano. The player, who was yet to be discovered, would one day become an icon. Chatter filled the air.

It was the end of a busy week in the early days of film production. Most everyone in attendance would one day stake a claim to fame or infamy. Some would go as high as you could go in "the business" at that time while others would begin their ascent only to fall hard.

Representing the ranks of both the highs and lows were Doris and Desiree. Desiree was a gorgeous red head with beautiful blue eyes and a willowy figure to match. Doris was a curvy blonde with an infectious laugh and an abundance of ambition. Doris had the drive to get to the top while Desiree's ambitions were often more modest.

Ironically, it was Desiree who found success first in films, followed by radio and eventually in television. Doris' drive was distracted by love and a crushing loss that sent her and her career into the depths of despair. Together, they started as "B" showgirls in the chorus of "A" list musicals just trying to get noticed by any studio executives.

They were seated at the ladies' room mirror applying touch-ups to their professionally made-up faces from work that day. They prepared themselves for an evening of wining and dining by a couple of self-professed, big-time producers. They'd never heard of these men before but they were just new enough to the industry to trust that these two shady characters might further their careers.

If nothing else, they would get a free meal from these gentlemen. As was the case for a struggling actress back in the day, you accepted invitations out of both the prospect of opportunity and the need to survive. Some gave up more than just their time to try to get ahead.

Neither Doris nor Desiree was the kind of lady who could be had for the mere price of a single meal. They both had talent and beauty working for them. It would be enough to open a few doors for each.

"Doris, where did you meet these two characters? They seem a little too fast talking for producers. Their clothes don't exactly scream success, either." Desiree said through pursed lips as she reapplied her lipstick. Doris replied while plucking her eyebrows and making faces of discomfort with each pluck. "I met them outside of props."

Desiree dabbed her lips with a handkerchief and proceeded to reposition strands of her hair, gluing them down with a lick of her own saliva. "Well, they could be anybody. We just need to look out for ourselves and each other. We came here together and we leave together. Agreed?" she said to Doris who replied, "Agreed, Desi!"

Comfortable with their appearance and ready for what the evening might bring, they proceeded to the dining room. Waiting anxiously were two young men trying their best to look prosperous while hoping that their dates ordered meals that they could afford. It was a sign of the still lingering depression that affected modest salaries.

The evening progressed nicely. Conversations volleyed between the men and the ladies as each were doing their best to determine if one side might get what they wanted from the other. Eventually, the hour was late and morning's call on set was early. The ladies gave their thanks while the true motives of the men became apparent.

"Thank you both for a lovely evening. We have an early call and need to get going." Desiree said as she gathered her purse and gave Doris a look signaling their need to exit. Doris had consumed just enough alcohol to afford her a look of desire for her handsome date.

"The night is young ladies. How about one drink at our place and then we'll drive you home?" Desiree's escort asked in an enticing tone. Doris looked at Desiree with the same hopeful gleam that a child would use to seek parental approval that would be denied.

"We'll have to do it another time. We have to be at the studio in six hours." Desiree replied as Doris donned a look of disappointment. "Call me!" Doris said to her date as Desiree tugged at her arm to lead her to the door, finalizing their departure with a, "Goodnight."

Weeks passed and for Desiree that one evening was gone and forgotten, as was her date. He was just another faux "producer" that seemed to plague Hollywood back in the early days. Back then, anyone could claim to help your career. Blind trust was rampant.

Doris, on the other hand, kept in contact with her date. They had gone out several times despite Desiree's discouragement. It was uncertain if Doris' interest in this man was love or lust. Desiree felt that he'd eventually be proven a cad and be gone but he did stay.

His name was Craig Hughes, or at least that was his stage name. It turned out that Desiree's suspicions were correct that he was not a producer. He was just another struggling actor but he had swarthy good looks and Doris' attention. They were soon to be in love.

Eventually, Doris and Craig married with Desiree as her Maid of Honor and Craig's cohort from their first date as his best man. It was a simple ceremony in a County office. Money was scarce but love abounded. Doris seemed so happy but Desiree held onto her doubts. She felt that Doris was moving much too quickly to marry.

Soon, one year had passed. Desiree continued to further her career. Doris would be sidetracked by the birth of her first child. It was a joyous arrival for Doris and Craig. Together, they took turns caring for their child as the other would accept any acting job to pay the bills. They didn't have much and would sometimes have to take odd jobs outside of acting to pay the bills but they had each other.

As Doris' career was stalled by the callings of family life, Desiree was making a true name for herself. Her big break came with one picture that had her playing a main character and getting rave reviews for it. It was a bitter pill to swallow for Craig and Doris to scrape together the price of two tickets to go see Desiree's new film.

As Doris sat in the theater looking up at her long-time friend's face larger than life on the screen, it stoked a twinge of jealousy. Her joy for Desiree was sincere, as was disappointment in her own career. Doris was not ready to surrender her dream and so she pressed on.

Months went by and like so many men during the early days of two world wars, Craig would be called to duty. Doris would mourn his departure out of fear for his life and the need for her son to have his father. Not long after Craig's enlistment into the military, Doris would learn that they were expecting their second child. Uncertain if she should wait, Doris wrote to Craig to advise of her pregnancy.

During Craig's departure, Doris suffered gladly through her share of responsibility. Her husband was gone and uncertain to return. She had to raise her son while preparing for another mouth to feed and she had to be bread winner for them all. Military pay being what it was back then, it was more of a supplement than a salary.

Doris reached out to her dear friend Desiree who had made quite a name for herself. Multiple film roles brought Desiree notoriety and prosperity. While seated in the living room of Desiree's palatial new home with her maid serving tea, Doris offered pleasantries as the introduction to her agenda. She needed Desiree's help to find work.

"Doris, you're looking a little tired. Is the little one keeping you up at night?" Desiree asked while stirring the cream into her tea with a short tap. Between being pregnant, keeping up with a lively toddler, the stress of a husband at war and the struggles of earning a living, Doris was more than a little tired. She was just barely hanging on.

"Desi, you're my closest friend and I feel that I can be honest with you. Things are tough right now and I need work. I thought maybe you could put in a good word for me at the studio. Maybe a small part in your next film?" Doris asked hoping for an old friend's offer of support. Desiree listened carefully while sipping her tea daintily.

"Of course, Doris. I'll see what I can find out for you in the morning. Until then, how about if I loan you some money to hold you over?" Desiree suggested as she walked to her desk and opened a drawer to retrieve her checkbook. It was tempting. Doris had urgent needs. "Well, I appreciate the offer but I'd rather work than borrow. If the studio doesn't have anything, perhaps I'll take you up on the offer of a loan later." Doris suggested. "Fair enough!" Desiree replied.

Days passed and Desiree called Doris to advise that she had spoken with the producer and director of her latest film. There was a small role with a few key lines being cast. Production was to begin in a few days. It wasn't much but it paid enough to hold Doris over for at least a few weeks until perhaps another role would present itself.

Doris knew that she'd have to make this money stretch as she was beginning to show. As was the case for any Hollywood production, a woman known to be pregnant was not considered employable. In an effort to conceal her maternal state, Doris had not even confided in Desiree out of fear that any opportunity might evaporate.

Doris managed to convince her mother to care for her son while she made her way to the studio for hair, make-up and costume. Upon arrival, she found herself being treated like any other bit player on the set while Desiree had a dressing room, an assistant and clout. It was not an easy situation for Doris to accept given the fact that she and Desiree started together but she was truly grateful for the job.

Doris' scenes were completed after a few days. She received her pay and returned to her life as an expectant mother with a husband in the war. As she neared the end of her pregnancy, Doris received word that her husband had been injured and would be sent home.

The immediate worry over his condition took away from what should have been a joyous time of reunion. Doris prepared for his eventual return to their modest home. Upon arrival in town, he was first sent to a hospital for rehabilitation and recovery of his injuries.

Doris was notified that Craig had arrived at the hospital. She hurried to greet him with their three-year old son. She stopped at a desk to seek directions to her husband's room. Once there, she was taken aback by his condition. He had scars on his face and a waist high cast on one leg. He was medicated and barely coherent.

Doris stood in the doorway holding her son's hand as he seemed hesitant to greet his father. "Doris?" he said in a faint whisper. Doris fought back tears of joy and sorrow while hurrying to his bed side.

Relieved for his safe return, Doris embraced her injured husband with the love of a devoted spouse. "Welcome home, Daddy!" his son said in his tiny voice. Doris lifted their son onto Craig's bed so that father and son could be reunited. Ravages of war were obvious on his body but his pride would prove to be the most affected.

After Craig's release from the hospital, he returned home to begin trying to piece together his life and his career. Unfortunately, his good looks that opened doors prior to his service were now scarred and lacking in the studio appeal required for a return to lead roles. He was no longer offered romantic roles of a dashing young man.

Now, he would only be offered roles as thugs and mobsters who donned stereotypical scarred faces. Rough looking and tough talking villains became his only offers but he needed to work. Between auditions, Craig began to fall prey to the demon drink to ease his pain of a permanent limp and a face that scared his son.

It wasn't long before Craig's drinking escalated into a problem that impaired his ability to show-up for auditions. Financial needs grew to the point that he had to take a job as a delivery person to pay the bills. Doris gave birth to their second child and had not worked in months. However, once the baby was old enough, she would again contact Desiree to seek assistance in securing any available roles.

Desiree had met and married a handsome, Latin actor named Rico. During their early years of marriage, Desiree and Rico were both busy working on films. Their time together was very limited. The Hollywood rumor mill had Rico seeing other women. Desiree could not tolerate a cheating spouse. She made an unusual career decision.

Avoiding divorce, Desiree secured an opportunity to work with her husband on a new radio program. In the eyes of Hollywood, she was going in the opposite direction. Most radio stars hoped for a film career but Desiree needed to save her marriage and she did.

Together, Desiree and Rico became radio's favorite husband and wife with Doris playing the nosey neighbor. It was Doris' big break.

The success of "My Favorite Life" grew. Doris was finally making a name for herself. Craig's despair was resolved daily at the bottom of a bottle. All too frequently, Doris came home from work only to find her husband in a drunken stupor with the kids hungry and dirty. "I'm not your maid!" he'd respond to her daily complaints.

It was now the mid-1950s. Masculine pride being what it was, Craig could not accept the demise of his acting career while his wife's was beginning to ascend. She begged him to stop drinking. He refused at every turn. After more than a year since Craig's last acting job, he surrendered to reality by quitting acting to become a postman. After less than a year on the job, he was fired for showing up drunk.

Doris continued her role on the radio gladly playing second fiddle to Desiree's character. However, over time, the stress of an alcoholic husband and an obvious need for a divorce took its toll on Doris. One would think that seeing her husband spiral into oblivion due to alcoholism would have been reason enough to avoid drinking.

Unfortunately, being part of the cocktail generation, her daily stress was eventually attended to using the same detrimental efforts that Craig used. Doris found herself having a little "nip" for various reasons large and small. If Craig was having a drink, she'd drink with him to keep him company. If her kids were behaving badly or work was stressful, she'd ease the pain with a strong bottle of relief.

While performing on the radio, Desiree began to notice that Doris would flub a line or slur her words. She often smelled of alcohol. It became increasingly obvious to Desiree, who was the producer, and to the sponsors that Doris needed to be shown the light or the door.

As fate would have it, just about the time that Doris was at grave risk of being replaced, television came calling to turn their program into a weekly comedy show. Doris was thrilled at the prospect of being a television star even if it was in Desiree's shadow. Upon learning of the news, Doris hurried home to tell Craig. By this time, Craig could no longer be trusted alone with their kids. While Doris worked, her mother was caregiver affording Craig privacy to drink.

Doris arrived mid-day to find Craig halfway to inebriation and less than friendly. "The show's headed to television. This is a huge break for me…for us." she said to a less-than enthusiastic spouse. He looked at her through bloodshot eyes and filled with envy. "Yeah, it's a huge break for 'US'!" he replied sarcastically.

Hearing of Doris' big break while knowing that he was more of a "never was" than a "has been" was more than Craig could endure. He downed his cocktail, grabbed his keys and headed for the door. When Doris got the part on Desiree's show, she gave her husband a grand gift of a motorcycle offered as a sign of increasing prosperity.

Doris stood staring out the window as Craig saddled onto his gift. The deafening roar of the powerful motor rang out until it could be heard no more as he made his way away from their home. Doris stood there saddened by her husband's sense of failure and by his lack of enthusiasm for her career. She took up where he left off.

Pouring herself a large tumbler of bourbon, Doris sat alone at the kitchen table wondering what to do about Craig. The irony was that she and her husband were both in need of recovery but she was in denial of her own alcoholism. Suddenly, the phone rang. Doris went to answer it only to be surprised by hearing Desiree's friendly voice.

"Doris, do you have a minute that I could speak with you about the show?" Desiree asked. Anxious to hear the details of their transition from radio to television, Doris replied, "Of course! I'm excited to get started in television. I've only done television a couple of times but I'm sure we'll adjust." Silence fell over Desiree's end of their chat.

Desiree finally spoke out, "Well, there's something that you should know. Your role has been filled by another actress. It wasn't my decision. It was a decision made by the network and the sponsors. They've been listening to your performances and felt that they couldn't take a chance on using someone with a drinking problem. It might hurt the show." Doris was speechless at the news that her first big break on screen was not going to happen. "We'll have a lot of character parts where we could really use you." Desiree added.

It was Doris' turn to fall silent. In that moment, Doris realized that she did have a drinking problem. Knowing that she would need to work, she did not want to express anger toward her friend and, potentially, future boss. "I understand. Of course, I'll gladly do any role that helps the show." Doris said with feigned sincerity.

"I'm very sorry. You know that I'd rather have you there with me." Desiree said sweetly. "I know. Thank you for including me in any possible way. I'll do my best in wrapping up the radio show." Doris added. Mutual gratitude was shared between them and the call ended. Doris' eyes filled with tears as she broke down in sorrow.

Following one of her life's greatest disappointments, Doris took all of the remaining liquor bottles and poured them down the drain. She had seen all too often from Craig just how easily alcohol can consume one's life. She refused to be next. Her battle of the bottle was over and, to her, Craig was to be confronted on his drinking.

Doris sat up waiting for Craig's return until she couldn't fight off sleep any longer. The rising sun began to shine in the window waking her and welcoming another day. Only today, Doris was determined that this was going to be a turning point in her life with Craig. What she wouldn't know yet was just how it would change.

Forcing herself to start the day, Doris made a strong pot of coffee. It was her plan to confront Craig with an ultimatum of either be sober or be single. No exceptions! She rehearsed her speech to herself repeatedly until she felt she was ready. Suddenly, the doorbell rang.

Opening the door, Doris was greeted by two police officers. "Is this the home of Craig Hughes?" an officer asked. "Yes! Is he in trouble? I'm his wife." Doris explained. "May we come in?" the officer asked as he removed his hat. "Of course. What's wrong?" Doris replied.

The officers proceeded to explain that Craig had been involved in a head-on collision between his motorcycle and a large truck. He was killed instantly. Lab tests concluded that his blood alcohol level was triple that of what the law considered reasonable back in the 1950s.

The day of Craig's funeral arrived. Doris stood graveside gripping her two young sons'. The younger boy didn't seem to understand that his father was not returning. Time would bring that reality. Reporters gathered nearby not because of Craig's previous films but because of Desiree's presence. Doris looked defeated by her loss.

Within the course of a week, Doris lost her husband and her one big career break. Although turning to drinking was tempting, she never again touched alcohol. She now had her sons to raise. She was not going to risk them losing another parent. They needed each other.

Doris did her best to meet the responsibilities of a single parent. It was in an era when most people assumed a woman could only survive if she were taken care of by a man. Doris was aging quickly. Her looks had served her well in her younger years but they were now fading fast. The number of potential suitors would be very few.

She had gained considerable weight and her appearance was that of a single working mother, not a Hollywood actress. The pitfalls of aging not so gracefully all but closed the door on her acting career. Doris had no choice but to take outside jobs to make ends meet.

One day, Doris was working at a laundry service. It was hard work for very little money. The setting was a steamy room crowded with bags of strangers' unmentionables. The stench of chemicals filled the air as she did her best to keep up with endless rows of ironing.

As fate would have it, the pressing room had a large glass window that faced the road next to a traffic light. Desiree was on her way to the studio one morning when her limousine stopped for a red light. Desiree happened to glance over and, much to her surprise, there was Doris. Her hair was wilted by steam and the oppressive heat.

Desiree's love and concern for her dear friend had her wanting to stop and offer assistance. She was humbled by Doris' ability to do just about anything to survive. However, Desiree considered how she would feel if the situation were reversed. It was her opinion that she'd want privacy and so privacy is what she afforded Doris.

Upon arrival at the studio, Desiree had her usual morning meetings to discuss details of her now wildly popular television show. While meeting with the writers and producer, Desiree advised that she wanted Doris to be cast in as many of the character roles that the show could possibly offer. She knew Doris would prefer a job over a loan. Doris was eventually cast in several cameo speaking roles. It paid the bills and she was glad to have the chance to act again.

Several weeks and several shows after Doris' debut as a laundress, Desiree invited her to tea. After the usual moments of rumors and reminiscence, Desiree made a big announcement to Doris. "You may have heard that Rico and I are branching out and producing a new show." Doris seemed surprised, "No, I've not heard about it."

Desiree continued, "It's a comedy about rural America. Two of the main characters are a farmer and his wife. We don't have a title yet but I'd like to offer you the role of the wife. You interested?" Doris looked delighted, if not relieved, to have steady work. "I'm in and thank you for considering me. You know I don't drink anymore?" she said in her most humble of voices. "I know!" Desiree replied.

Reflecting upon her discovery of Doris' job at the laundry, Desiree wanted to offer her support. It was important to her that Doris knew that she could count on her in any time of need. Their careers may have taken two different directions but their origins were solid.

Seeking satisfaction of curiosity, Desiree said, "Doris, I want to ask you about something. I was riding to work one day and I saw you working in a laundry. Why didn't you call me if you needed work? You know I'd help." Doris looked a bit embarrassed knowing that her friend had seen her in a moment of surviving necessity. "I didn't want to bother you. You're a big star now. You're busy and I didn't want to take up your time." she replied with a weepy face.

Desiree looked insistent in her response, "Doris, you're my dearest friend. I know that I'm lucky to be where I am but my good fortune started with you. You're like family. I'll always have time for you!" Doris' tears were now inevitable. "Thank you!" she said sincerely.

After the reaffirmation of their long-held bond, Desiree continued to captivate America with her weekly escapades. Doris began work on her new show as the farmer's dowdy wife. It was a show that had a silly premise but became a hit. It brought to Doris something that she had never known before; notoriety but without true fame.

On her first day on the set of her new show, Doris received a large bouquet of beautiful flowers and a gift box from Tiffany's. The card with the flowers read, "Break a leg…Love Desi and Rico!" Doris opened the box from Tiffany's and inside was a beautiful diamond encrusted watch. On the back, the inscription read, "I'll always have time for you! D." The love of a dear friend meant everything to her.

Doris' new series was well into a successful fourth season when she would face her greatest challenge. Illness would pervade Doris' life. Her sons were now grown and she was in her early fifties. Doris' expanding waist line and high blood pressure caused heart disease.

She collapsed one day on the set. Upon arrival at the hospital, she was told to get her final affairs in order. The limits of medicine in the 1960s were such that there was little hope. In her final days, Doris called Desiree to say goodbye. Desi hurried to the hospital.

She arrived at the hospital to find Doris' sons sitting with her looking somber and lost. Despite her struggles, Doris had always been a kind and loving mother. Desiree sat on the edge of Doris' bed holding her hand. Doris faded into a peaceful slumber until a doctor arrived, checked her pulse and confirmed her final demise.

Despite her success, Desiree always made time for Doris in her life and in her final moments. Some successful actresses might have discarded the individuals that were with them on their rise to fame. Desiree stayed loyal because she owed a debt of gratitude to Doris.

Doris was offered a lucrative role early on in her career. She turned it down because she felt it would leave Desiree behind. It was an act of selflessness that Doris failed to keep secret from Desiree. Later, Desiree accepted the same role. It launched her career into stardom.

Chapter 2

Throwing a Stone

The sounds of feminine giggling whispered into young Josh's ear as he strolled by two enamored girls in the hallway of his high school. Teenage girls giving him stares and whispering to each other was a familiar event. Josh's wholesome good looks afforded him the envy of the boys and the amorous desires of most of the girls in school.

They were all part of a 1950s graduating class with mere days left before they were off to begin their adult lives. No more reigning parental authority. No more adolescent expectations to be met by the orders of high school teachers, coaches and administrators. Life was making its grand turn to adulthood with angst of the unknown.

Everyone was making plans for their summer celebrations as they anticipated the impending graduating ceremony. Josh's friend since early elementary school was an average looking guy with ulterior motives. Burt was his name and he enjoyed being Josh's sidekick. Josh assumed that Burt liked the parade of girls surrounding him in school. He'd never know that Burt really had a secret crush on him.

These two friends had a long history but their futures were headed in two very different directions. Burt's life would be limited to living in his parents' guest house while attending a local college. Josh was from a family of modest means. Paying for college was a struggle. Higher education was vacated for his Hollywood dream.

Josh's passion was to be an actor. He had the desire, persistence and good looks that would serve him well. Talent was secondary to his classic, chiseled features. He also had an advantage that other actors did not. He looked very much like a well-known actor from a popular television show named Dirk Roark. It opened a few doors.

Once he arrived in Hollywood, Josh would often be stopped and asked for his autograph from fans thinking that he was Dirk. The struggles of his beginnings were familiar to any actor starting out. During his early years, like so many others, Josh had to earn a living between acting jobs. It was the proverbial, ongoing issue of "feast or famine". Funds were either abundant or scarce as Josh worked just about any job trying to pay for acting classes, rent and feed himself.

There were the legitimate producers who would do callbacks that provided of a week or more of work. Perhaps a small role on a drama or a sitcom. Just enough to help build a resume. Then, there were the smarmy types that always seemed to want to meet in more remote locations, such as motels and warehouses. All under the premise of a low budget but a good role if he would just cooperate.

With obvious motives, those with the lesser budgets frequently had a need to see him in a state of undress. He'd be stripped down to his underwear, in a swimsuit or just a small towel wrapped around him. Josh became very good at spotting the leads of legitimacy versus the signs of impropriety, such as fees they paid to see skin.

Some actors had given-in to deceit and desperation. On occasion, Josh had even been known to remove the towel to give a so-called producer a good look and collect his "audition fee". However, a long stare was as far as he'd go nor would he ever allow pictures. Considering that homosexuality was mostly illegal, it was alive and well and thriving in those early days of Hollywood debauchery.

It would take some time but eventually Josh had made enough of a name for himself that his agent would arrange all meetings. Once a professional took over the reigns of opportunity, the sleazy element from the bowels of Hollywood were no longer a necessity for Josh.

As was the case for many young actors in the mid-century days of Hollywood, studios sought to change his name to match his strong, on-screen image. Josh Ellstrom soon became Jack Stone without any hesitation. His parents weren't happy with the change but he was. It didn't take long before Jack was embraced and Josh was discarded.

His first big break came playing a small but semi-frequent role on a weekly sitcom. As the brother-in-law of the lead character, Jack was a familiar sight for family and friends each week on television. For Burt, it was surreal to see his friend from first grade playing a role on one of his favorite shows. For Josh's parents, it brought bragging rights. For Jack, it brought the chance to make a name for himself while earning a living in the make-believe world of his big dream.

Time passed and Jack's show was renewed for a second season despite a lag in the ratings. The social climate of the mid-1960s was experiencing considerable change. Drugs, free love and long hair on men became more true-to-life than suits and greased manes. The squeaky-clean image of young people portrayed on television was now inaccurate. The show was about young people whose lives no longer matched the real world. This format was at the end of an era.

The overall ratings of the show held strong enough to justify a third season. However, the show's star wanted out to do better projects. It meant that Jack's steady job was coming to an end but that was just the nature of show business. He'd press-on and find other work.

Almost immediately, he landed on another sitcom but it was so bad it was cancelled after only a few episodes. There were a couple of low budget films that he did because of his resemblance to Dirk Roark. The films' producers never would have procured Dirk for the kind of money they were paying or with such bad scripts. Jack didn't care if he was a pale imitation of a big star. He needed work.

Eventually, Jack was lured back to television with an audition to play a lead character in a unique western premise. The show used the familiar western genre but added a comedic flair that audiences found appealing. It was also a show that was originally intended for Dirk Roark but he was still under contract with another show.

"Smith and Wesson" became wildly popular despite a decline in the western genre. The show featured Jack and another very handsome actor in the lead roles. Together, they seemed to have a comedic chemistry that appealed to all ages and both genders equally.

Back home, the barrage of friends and family were still in awe of Jack's (Josh's) success. Burt had finished college but was still living with his mother after his father's untimely death. Jack's parents made sure that everyone knew that was their son on television. Jack loved his show and all of the perks that came with it. From the endless supply of pretty girls to the fancy home and car he sported, Jack seemingly had everything going for him until fate came calling.

It was tragedy in pairs that brought misfortune. First, Jack's mother took ill and died very suddenly. Apparently, cancer had spread throughout her body as a result of undiagnosed breast cancer. It was mere weeks between diagnosis and death. Jack was devastated and had to miss filming his show to attend his mother's funeral.

Upon arrival in town for the service, Jack found himself in the middle of a media frenzy. The local media and dozens of fans were staked outside of his parents' home night and day just to see a star. It was as if his mother's death didn't matter to these people. It was the first time in his career that he bemoaned the pitfalls of success.

Fortunately, his good friend Burt came to the rescue. After Burt's father passed away, financial need forced Burt to move out of their guest house to make way for paying tenants. The most recent tenant had recently departed and the guest house was temporarily vacant. Jack hid out to avoid the press and fans insensitive to his recent loss.

The second streak of bad luck was that rumors were flying around that Dirk Roark wanted off of his current show. If he could get out of his contract, there was a good chance that Jack's producers would want Dirk to replace him. Afterall, he was a bigger name and the resemblance between the two would make for a seamless transition.

Jack decided to take matters into his own hands and made his way onto the set of Dirk's show. While filming wrapped for the day the cast and crew were making their way off the lot. Jack found Dirk's dressing room, knocked and waited to hear, "It's open!" from Dirk.

Jack entered the grander surroundings of a bigger star. "Dirk, you probably don't know me but my name is..." he said until Dirk interrupted. "Jack Stone! I wondered how long it would be before we came face to face since we apparently have the same face." Dirk said with a friendly smile and his hand extended to shake Jack's.

Jack was taken by surprise. He expected a big confrontation, not a friendly welcome. "Nice to meet you." Jack said as he shared a tight grip with his well-known doppelganger. "Have a seat." Dirk said.

Together, they sat sipping beers and making small talk about the industry until the reason for Jack's visit surfaced in conversation. "Dirk, I came to see you because I've been hearing rumors that you might be leaving this show to replace me on mine. Is this true?" Jack asked politely while holding onto hope that it was false publicity.

Dirk finished his beer while looking pensive as to how he could best answer the question without upsetting anyone. He opted for nothing less than a direct approach, "Honestly, nothing has been decided but I don't think you have anything to worry about. Jerry Ackert is the executive producer on my show. He's probably going to take over as executive producer over on your set. He came to me recently and told me that if he does go to your show, he wants me to take over your role." Jack was now showing obvious concern.

"Are you going to do it?" Jack asked. "Jerry has a plan. He wants us to switch shows. He wants you to take my place on this show. He knows that if they don't let me out of my final year here, I'm going to leave when my year is up. If you're on the other show, they can't use you to continue this one and your show is too popular to cancel. If we switch roles, I get out of here, the two shows continue and the audiences barely notice the switch." Dirk explained to a silent Jack.

At this point Dirk knew that he had probably shared more than he should have without any official announcements being made. He was seemingly doing his best to honor actor comradery. "Jack, as far as I'm concerned, you have nothing to worry about. I've seen your show and I think you're perfect for it. Besides, I don't want to do a western. I have other offers. Even if I have to do another year here, I'll have something else waiting for me." Dirk said assuredly.

The friendly banter of what Jack felt was a newly formed friendship continued until it was time to wish each other well. Jack left the set feeling certain that his job was safe. Time passed and Jack returned to work. He felt a bit distracted by his mother's death and Dirk's declaration but he told nobody. One day, it was announced that the show had a new boss, Jerry Ackert. The big surprise came when Jerry advised that Dirk was joining the show as Jack's older brother.

Jack was speechless and confused since there were no discussions of him leaving the show to make way for Dirk. No discussions until Dirk's first script was out. Jack thumbed through the script to find that his character was being killed off. He was uncertain of what he was more upset over; his character's demise or Dirk's lies to him.

Clutching his script, Jack stormed into Jerry's office to find his new boss sitting and laughing with his "big brother". Jack slammed the script down on Jerry's desk and began to rant, "What the hell is this? You're killing off my character without even telling me?" Dirk looked at Jerry with an insulting smirk on his face. "Calm down, you still have a job. We're sending you over to Dirk's show to play his role." Jerry explained in his raspy, cigar toking producer's voice.

Jack was defiant, "The hell I am! I have a contract with this show and I intend to stay here until it's done. I'll ask my attorney to call you to explain how contracts work." Jerry chuckled at Jack's feeble attempt to intimidate and replied, "You might want your attorney to explain to you how a contract works. You're not under contract with the show. You're under contract with the studio and we can use you in any show we choose. If you don't meet the contract, you'll be sued and if that happens, no studio will ever hire you."

Jack looked to Dirk for any signs of support displayed during their previous conversation but he was smugly silent. "So, I guess your speech about not wanting to do a western was bullshit?" Jack asked of Dirk who replied, "I'm in the same boat as you, kid. I have to go where they tell me to go. There's nothing we can do!" Jack stormed out to call his attorney who confirmed Jerry's contractual claim.

The mood on set was pervaded by unfriendly interaction between Dirk and Jack. Lines were read and parts were played until it was time for the final scene. The script called for the demise of Jack's character by way of a shooting where he falls off of a horse. The stunt double was held up on another set and there was only the final shot to make to wrap up filming. Jack was told to make the fall onto an off-camera landing of foam pads. Reluctantly, he complied but the horse turned. Jack made a hard landing missing the pads.

Jack spent the next few weeks attempting recovery of a severe back injury. Making matters worse was the studio's insurance company who blamed him for the injury. They stated that he performed a stunt for which he "was untrained and should have refused." If he had refused, he wasn't meeting his contract. It was a dispute that left Jack unable to work and stuck paying substantial medical bills.

As the end of summer hiatus approached, Jack was due on set with Dirk's former show to resume his role. Upon arrival, he was greeted by a less-than friendly co-star whose husband was also the director and one of the producers. Beth Ashmont was the opposite of her sweetly dispositioned character. She was also upset by the change in cast that was protested but she and her husband were overruled.

Filming began on Jack's new show while he was propped up with a back brace. Believability of his character was forced through a haze of pain killers. Production was well into the season's lengthy thirty-two episodes when Jack collapsed into a seizure. Production was halted and reruns aired as the show's producers decided what to do. Jack eventually returned on a limited basis shooting his scenes sitting down but it just wasn't working. The physicality of the character was not being met by a man who was always seated.

Much to his disappointment, Jack's contract was paid out. He was being replaced by the Beth's original choice who was previously unavailable. After only a few years of being a successful actor, Jack was now at home, in pain and unemployed for an indefinite period.

Fortunately, the studio insurance company settled his injury claim. Between the insurance money, his contract pay-out and years of being a well-paid actor, he didn't have to be concerned about money but his spirit was broken. He fell into a deep depression exacerbated by drinking and a prescription pain killer addiction.

One day, Jack was in need of attending a doctor's appointment for a surgical consultation. His hope was that surgery would take away his ongoing agony of back pain. He should have taken a taxi due to his intoxication. Instead, he made a bad decision to drive himself.

Attempting to make his way to the doctor, Jack weaved down the road until he somehow managed to arrive alive. It was a commute that posed great danger to himself and everyone along his route. Not feeling that he was unfit to drive, Jack ignored obvious signs.

After meeting with the doctor, the potential for resolution to Jack's back injury was minimal at best. He left the office disappointed that surgery was unlikely to take away his pain. His goal was to be well enough to return to acting before his name faded from the industry. In Hollywood, absence causes one's fame to fade faster than it came.

He hopped into his sports car and pulled away from the curb while still feeling the effects of his morning pain pill mixed with a Bloody Mary. While attempting to stop at a traffic light, Jack mistakenly pressed the gas instead of the brake. The car suddenly bolted into the crosswalk knocking two people to the ground causing injuries.

As a crowd gathered, Jack hurried to aid his victims. "Somebody, please call for an ambulance." he yelled as he looked at the bloodied faces and torn clothing of two innocent people. It wasn't long before the sounds of sirens approached. The victims were carried away for medical attention but Jack had questions to answer for the police.

The attending officer noticed that Jack's speech was slurred and inquired as to his sobriety. "I'm on some prescription medication but no, I'm not drunk, if that's what you're asking." Jack replied defensively. Objecting to the officer's insinuations, Jack was taken into custody on the officer's suspicion of driving while impaired.

While being booked, for the first time ever, someone recognized Jack Stone as a celebrity. Back in his hometown, he was besieged with requests for autographs. However, in Hollywood, a mistaken request for Dirk Roark's autograph had always been Jack's burden. It was untimely irony that the booking officer wanted an autograph.

After being released, Jack returned home to process that his once promising career and gilded life were now starting to crumble. One injury had taken away his health, his career and soon his money.

It didn't take long after the accident before the lawsuits arrived. Auto insurance back in the 1960s was very limited but the claims were substantial. Medical bills, lost wages, permanent disabilities. It all added up very quickly and would take the vast majority of Jack's money to settle. He was left strapped for cash and unemployable.

Eventually, Jack had to sell his palatial home in order to survive. He moved into a very modest apartment while he continued to do what he could to earn a living. His manager was able to arrange a few radio commercials but the pay was a fraction of his previous salary.

As if his financial losses and health were not enough to handle, yet another life changing event would happen. Jack's friend Burt called late one evening to advise of his father's death after he fell in the tub, hit his head and drowned. Burt had been aiding in the father's care in Jack's absence and made the gruesome discovery.

Jack hurried back to his hometown to arrange a funeral that he was struggling to afford. His father's house would be the only asset left behind. Despite Jack's generosity to his parents over the years, the house was in a state of disrepair and held very little value. Jack was considering moving back from Hollywood to live in the house.

Afterall, his parents were dead and so was his career. What reason did he have to remain in Hollywood? Jack decided he would return to Hollywood for one final attempt at resurrecting a once promising career. He gave up drinking and pain killers to bring a focus that only sobriety could offer. He attempted to strengthen his back and tone his body at his local gym. He made every effort to recover.

After a few weeks, Jack was showing signs of improvement. He went to see his manager who had all but given up on him. After a lengthy discussion, the manager said that he would do his best to find Jack work suitable for his experience and he almost succeeded.

Jack was called in to audition for much-hyped, big budget picture. It was the kind of opportunity Jack's career had never achieved. The producers seemed to like his read. Things looked very promising.

Much to Jack's surprise and delight, he was cast in this expensive saga. It was to be his comeback and his greatest role as a leading man. Production began and the schedule was grueling. Long days on location during a very hot summer were taking a toll on the set.

Take after take were demanded by the director who seemed happy with everyone's performance, except Jack's. Jack did his best to deliver his lines but the director never seemed satisfied. It was all Jack could do to hold his temper but he needed this film to succeed.

Production was halted for an undisclosed reason. The entire cast were uncertain as to why they were waiting. Jack was at his hotel expecting a call to set when the phone rang. It was the executive producer who casually announced that Jack was being replaced by, none other than, Dirk Roark. Jack was devastated by the news.

Returning home with prorated pay and the humiliation of having to tell everyone that he was fired, Jack fell into the depths of despair. It was bad enough that his career was not being jumpstarted but to have Dirk Roark yank the rug out one more time was just too much.

Months passed and the holidays were upon him. Jack had spent those months trying to get any substantial opportunity to act again. He begged his manager to secure a sitcom, drama, low-budget film, anything but there were no takers. No auditions. Nothing to offer.

News Year's eve had arrived and what few friends Jack had did their best to snap him out of his blue funk. Knowing of his sobriety, these friends should have celebrated without alcohol but forgot. Jack was invited to attend a big bash where he became intoxicated. Friendly reassurances of better days to come only made it worse.

Not feeling in a celebratory mood, Jack took a taxi home before midnight. Once home, he turned on the television to watch people celebrating their joy when he had none. Emotions washed over him. After a brief deliberation, he went to his closet to find his gun. Tears poured from his eyes as he put the gun to his head and hesitated. He almost stopped but pulled the trigger. His body fell to the floor.

The next morning was the first day of a new year. Burt was up early at home sipping his coffee until he decided to retrieve the morning newspaper. While still fighting the effects of sleep, Burt unfolded the course feeling paper that was about to change his world forever. "Local Actor Commits Suicide" the headline shockingly delivered.

Burt sat with tears streaming down his face as his mother, Rose, entered the kitchen. Together, they mourned the loss of the young boy who had once sat in that same kitchen laughing as a child. It was a tragic and surreal way to start a new year for mother and son.

Months passed since Jack's untimely death rocked a small town and a big industry. Burt and everyone who loved Jack was doing their best to recover from the unanswered question of "Why?" The film that Jack was fired from was released and, as Jack suspected, was a huge hit. Dirk Roark was nominated for acting's highest honor.

As fate would have it, Dirk won this prestigious award for a role that Jack needed to be his victory. In his acceptance speech, Dirk had either the class or the gall to acknowledge Jack. Dirk went on to sing the praises of a fellow actor that he beat out at every turn. Perhaps it was the nature of a cutthroat industry. Perhaps Dirk just wanted to honor a friend. True intentions would remain a mystery.

Despite their years of living two very different lives, Burt never lost his love and respect for Josh. Josh Ellstrom and Jack Stone may have shared a body but they were never the same person to Burt. Jack was a talented, ambitious person who saw his dream and did his best to claim it. Some may say he failed but others knew how hard it was to accomplish as much as Jack managed to achieve in his life.

Josh was the little boy that Burt met in first grade who played with him when the other kids called him a sissy. Josh taught Burt how to ride a bike and how to swim. Josh was the one who said nothing to anyone when Burt allowed his crush on Josh to surface long enough to plant a kiss on his lips. Other boys would have ruined Burt over a kiss but Josh laughed it off. It was an innocent act of friendship between two kids exploring life through the joys of make-believe.

Chapter 3

A Star is Mourned

Melody Bliss stands posed ever-so-carefully while donning her best Hollywood stage face readying herself for the blinding photo ops. The paparazzi clamored for her attention as the fans pleaded for a wave. She blew a kiss of feigned sincerity in their general direction.

This was a big night for Miss Bliss, as she insisted on being called. Bliss being a definite improvement over her birth name of Melanie Drumpf. This nomination for a coveted "Marlon" award places her second behind Lydia Carlisle in terms of nominations but no wins.

Continuing her sashay down the red carpet, she headed toward the double-doored ingress of the opulent awards theater. "Please, don't let me run into Lydia. PLEASE, don't let me run into Lydia." she whispered to herself. She was almost there. Just a couple more feet and she'd be inside. "Melody, there you are. I've been looking for you. I really want to wish you just, so much...luck!" Lydia said through obvious and thinly-veiled insincerity. Melody smiled back.

Lydia Carlisle was the unstoppable queen of cinematic awards. She held the record for the most nominations and wins for every major award in Hollywood. She was a master of accents, astonishing at defining characters and an absolute genius at recreating real people. She had to be a great actress because her public believed her to be sweet. Lydia Carlisle was Beelzebub in Dior. Vicious and good at it.

If there was a female role worth having, she wanted it and she'd stop at nothing to get it. If a soft approach didn't work for Lydia, bullying would. Despite Melody having a fair amount of talent of her own, Lydia Carlisle was the Marlon winner more often than not.

Melody almost won during a year that Lydia lost a role to an icon who hadn't made a film in years. Lydia took a role in an indie film and was nominated. Unfortunately for Lydia and Melody, that same year, that iconic actress won posthumously. As voting grew near, she had a fatal peanut allergy attack after having lunch at Lydia's. Anything for a win, except Lydia didn't win. She did play her greatest role ever at the cemetery throwing herself on the casket. Melody stood graveside underwhelmed by Lydia's overacting.

Melody made her way to her second-row seat. Of course, it was directly behind Lydia's front-row seat. As their category was to be called, Melody looked around for her missing husband, Drake. He, too, was an actor but not of the same caliber as his famous spouse.

At times, it created hostility as Drake resented being asked to step aside for a fan's photo or being called, "Mr. Bliss". He had stunning looks but lacked any real talent. When Drake and Melody met, she saw someone who looked good on her arm in a publicity photo. He saw opportunity. Eventually, they married but it was never for love.

Just as they were to announce the nominees, Drake arrived out of breath and fixing his hair. "You have a spot of something on you." she said while rolling her eyes. Drake looked down only to find rather conspicuous proof of infidelity. It was in the form of a glob of a certain bodily fluid that men leave behind after a good time. "Oh, I sneezed a minute ago. How embarrassing." he said nervously.

Melody was focused on her win, not his wad. The winner was to be announced and Melody was on the edge of her seat. "Not Lydia. PLEASE not Lydia!" she whispered to herself. "And the winner is…" said the presenter. The audience fell silent. "Melody Bliss" rang out from the podium microphone. "Who's she? Oh, that's me!" she thought as the audience stood in applause. Lydia looked bitter.

Melody turned to Drake for an obligatory kiss of congratulations. Not knowing where his mouth may have been recently, she turned her head to expose her cheek to his air kiss as she smiled and stood. The audience's adulation made the moment seem as if it were playing out in slow motion. Melody waved as she savored her win and then it happened. Our winner tumbled to the floor with her assets exposed to the cameras as the world looked on and gasped.

Perhaps it was her disorientation on her way down to humiliation. However, she seemed certain that just as her face hit the floor and her feet hit the air, a peripheral view of a black pump retracting from the front row seemed apparent. "Oh, Mel! Are you okay?" Lydia asked. Melody righted herself and gathered her dignity.

Her nosedive from nowhere only added to the audience's ovation. Melody gave her oration of thanks without any further incident. Later that evening, after making victorious rounds to the numerous parties, Melody and Drake returned to their separate lives at home.

Placing her golden accolade on the mantel for central viewing, Melody hummed to herself as Drake stood seething in jealousy. He knew the chances of him ever having the same honor were slim-to-none. The last several years married to Marlon's latest winner was opportunity going nowhere fast. When he married, he assumed that being "Mr. Bliss" would open doors but it didn't. As far as Drake was concerned, it was time to find a new coattail to ride upon.

Months went by and Melody found her career to be stalled. After her glorious win, she assumed that offers would be replete and declinations at her discretion. Instead, as often happens to actors with a big win, studios and producers assumed she was out of their league. Lydia would prove to be the exception because she never made big demands or asked for big money. The role was her wage.

In an attempt to take a new approach to furthering her career, Melody sought new representation. They promised her results that never materialized. Nearly two years had passed since her last film. Melody found herself taking lesser roles in order to pay the bills.

Drake managed to secure a role on a soap opera and it was his first steady job since they married. For the first time, he was the primary breadwinner. If he made the money and got nothing for being "Mr. Bliss", why did he need her? He didn't sign-on to just be her spouse.

Drake's fame as an actor grew as hers as an actress took a dive. One day, the show's producer announced the leading lady was leaving. The producers needed a replacement. Someone who could play the role and bring something new to it. Someone with a big name and Drake had access to a big name. They wanted Melody to be the lead.

After having won the most prestigious award an actor could win, she wasn't interested in the role but needed work. She acquiesced.

Feeling the love from her new castmates, Melody arrived on-set to great fanfare. Flowers adorned her dressing room and her gay assistant, Joe, attended to her every whim. The attention paid to the new lead actress was more than well-received; it was overdue. After having been absent for years, maybe this gig wasn't so bad after all.

Melody brought to the show a new perspective. She was the consummate professional with a fresh approach to playing an iconic role as a family matriarch. Her character had a history of being the bitch and Melody continued that tradition. However, at Melody's suggestion, her character's softer side would make an occasional appearance. Not too frequently. Just enough to bring her likeability.

Drake's character, Dante, was the handsome billionaire to Melody's Deandra. It took every bit of talent that they both could engender to bring believability of a loving bond. Their real marriage was empty and plagued by rumors of divorce but money was a consideration.

Melody had now been on the show for over two years. The ratings were strong and the producers were happy. As is the case for the soap opera genre, ongoing change was needed to retain the viewers' interest. It was decided that a new character would be introduced. Drake battled Hollywood's demand for youth. The producers opted for a younger love interest for Deandra and he was muy caliente!

Tomas DelFuego was a former soap opera actor who made it big by becoming a singer. His singing career took off like a rocket mainly due to his gyrating dance moves that drove women, and a few men, crazy with sexual desire. After a few years, the scheduling demands of rigorous tours became too much. Tomas wanted his life back. He decided to make his return to acting. His draw would be a big name along with the looks required to fit into the cast and character.

Tomas played the Latin billionaire, Luis, who came to town with a hostile takeover of Dante's empire. Luis had the money, the muscles and a conspicuous bulge in his pants that wasn't his wallet. He oozed sex and power. It drove most of the audience and some of the cast wild with sexual desire. Melody's lust for Tomas was pulsating.

It didn't take long before Melody was more than distracted by the show's Latin heartthrob. She was obsessed with Tomas. She wanted him and she didn't care who knew. Drake could have his divorce, if he wanted it. Melody had serious delusions of grandeur as far as her belief that she and Tomas would one day be married. She believed that all she needed one opportunity to seduce Tomas.

Tensions on the set were such that Drake and Melody only spoke if their characters spoke to each other. Tomas was oblivious to all of the attention. He was just trying to do his job and get along with the cast and crew. Never did it occur to him that anyone desired him.

The first season with Tomas on set was soon to end. The summer hiatus would be the perfect time for Melody to launch her plan to capture Tomas' attention. She invited him out on the small yacht she had purchased after the show gave her a substantial bonus. The only flaw in her plan of seduction would be her husband who heard from Tomas about the invitation spending a weekend on the water.

Drake was surprised to hear that his wife was intending to host a guest without his knowledge. Not wanting to be left out or stepping aside for Melody's open affair, Drake opted for a surprise arrival on board their boat, appropriately named after Melody, the *"Blissful"*.

It was a beautiful Friday sunset when Melody and Tomas arrived to greet the captain. Melody's assistant, Joe, was onboard attending to their dinner and cocktails. "Dinner is served." Joe said with a smile. Melody held tightly to her cocktail but even tighter to the arm of an unsuspecting Tomas. They entered the dining room and much to Melody's surprise, the table was set for three to dine, but why?

"Joe, why are there three place settings?" Melody asked. Just then, Drake appeared from the galley door, "I thought I'd join you!" he said with a smirk. Unaware of Melody's intentions, Tomas smiled to greet Drake. Melody was shocked and miffed. Her plan was stymied and there was nothing she could do. "I'm so glad that you could join us." she said with feigned sincerity of an unexpected spouse. Together, they ate but Melody's plan was yet to squashed.

The evening ended with Tomas retiring to a guest room and Drake to his room. He and Melody had not shared a room for quite some time. The next two days were to be spent leisurely sailing around the California coast. Melody was determined to have Tomas despite Drake's presence. It was a sunny Saturday with cocktails being as plentiful as the ocean's wake. Tomas donned a skimpy bathing suit that added to Melody's lust. Drake was the ever-present intruder.

The return of an evening's sunset provided picturesque vistas of a soothing hue that set a mood. Inebriation was obvious by all three of the boat's residents. Dinner was shared, drinks were poured and all that was left was dessert. The late hour approached with the ship being moored and the crew being fast asleep. The evening became a drunken battle of who could hold out the longest, Melody or Drake.

Tomas had reached his limit of alcohol and animosity between the dueling detriment of two unhappily married hosts. He gave his thanks and retired to his quarters. Melody gave her most seething stare to her husband who had spoiled her plot. He downed his last cocktail and said, "I'm headed to bed, too." before leaving the room.

At this point, Melody was full-on drunk. She stood up but the rock of the boat nearly had her losing her balance. She staggered down the hall to her room. She wanted one final attempt to satisfy her lust for a sexy Latin lover. She brushed her hair, freshened her breath, slipped into a slinky gown and made her way to Tomas' quarters.

She pressed her ear against the door listening for sounds of him still being awake. She heard unidentifiable noise indicating that he must still be up. She tapped lightly on the door as not to get Drake's attention in the room next door but no answer. Turning the door knob quietly to give an element of surprise, the surprise was on her.

In the glow of a single light above the bed, there was Tomas naked, kneeling on the bed with his face to the ceiling while moaning. Melody looked down to see her husband's naked body and his head bobbing up and down directly in front of Tomas' crotch "Oh my God!" she shrieked as Drake grabbed the sheet to cover them both.

Melody bolted from the room running down the hallway and out to the deck. Still feeling the effects of severe intoxication, she found herself disoriented in the dark of night. She was looking for the crew quarters to tell the captain to return the boat to shore. Drake came running after her wearing only a towel. "Melody, WAIT!" he yelled in her direction as he began running toward her. She saw him and turned to find the steep stairs leading to the crew quarters.

Drake grabbed her arm and said, "I'm sorry. I thought you knew." Melody was seething in anger and feeling embarrassed. Her shock over the situation wasn't just because she saw her husband having sex with a man but also because she never questioned his sexuality. "Let me go! I don't want to talk to you right now." she insisted. "Let me go!" she yelled as she jerked her arm free from Drake's grasp.

"Come back to your cabin. We can talk about this." he pleaded. She was determined to not address the matter in that moment. "I'll talk to my divorce attorney but I'm not talking to you." she said as she proceeded to climb the narrow ladder heading to the crew quarters. The strong winds stole Drake's towel as he turned to go inside.

The waves of the ocean were creating a substantial wake. The night breeze was strong and Melody's sea legs were wobbly from the many cocktails throughout the day. She held on to the rail as she continued her ascent up the crew ladder. Suddenly, she was being forced off the ladder. She fought with all of her strength to hold on.

Her hands were freed either by mother nature's strong wind or the hand of someone with a motive for her to not reach the shore. In either case, she fell and struck her head on the ladder as she was tossed to the starboard railing. The boat was rocked by the wake. Melody was thrown overboard without making any yell for help.

Later, the break of an early morning sun rose over the ocean for the captain to admire as he exited his cabin to greet a new day. He stretched and looked for signs of others but the deck was empty. It was serenely quiet below as he looked down to find a lady's watch on the deck. The face was cracked and the time stopped at 3:33am.

That same morning, the captain of another boat three miles away was also making his way to the deck to greet the glowing sunrise of another beautiful day. He looked out at the sun's rays reflecting off of the glassy shimmer of an eerily calm ocean surrounding him.

While feeling the steam on his face from the sip of his first cup of morning motivation, he could see an unidentifiable object floating nearby. It was conspicuously out of place with a billowy exterior of pink blowing in the breeze at its edges. It appeared to be a large bird who had met its demise. The captain stared carefully placing his flatten fingers over his eyes to lessen the glare of the rising sun.

"What is that?" he said to himself. He reached for his binoculars. adjusting the sights until a clear image could be displayed. It was some kind of feathered-looking carcass catching an early breeze. He continued his gaze seeking any other signs of identification. Based on its size, it had to be a larger bird such as a flamingo or a pelican.

Doing his best to satisfy his curiosity as the boat made its subtle rock from the modest waves, the captain noticed what looked like hair floating in the wake. He could also see a lifeless arm and leg bobbing up and down to the water's repetitive motion. "Oh my, God!" he said as he hurried to pull the anchor and start the motor.

Steering the boat toward the body, he sounded the horn to awaken the boat's sleeping occupants for their assistance. Immediately, his wife arrived on deck soon followed by their two grown children. "Get on the radio and call for the Coast Guard." he said to his wife.

With his family looking on in horror, the boat slowly approached the unidentified body. The captain dropped anchor and grabbed a long pole from the deck pulling it closer to their swim platform. He reached down and with all of his strength he pulled onboard the heavy, bloated corpse of a woman dressed in a slinky pink negligee.

The daughter of the captain turned her head away as not to stare at the substantial wound on the woman's head or her eyes staring up. They waited anxiously for the Coast Guard to arrive and claim her.

The captain of the *Blissful* was listening at the ongoing chaos that ensued upon the Coast Guard's arrival at the other boat. As if he was listening to an old radio mystery unfolding, he was glued to the informational updates being dispersed to the sea-going community.

The call was for all vessels in the area to immediately confirm the presence of every passenger and report back on anyone who was missing. Following maritime rules, the captain proceeded to wake Melody's assistant, Joe, to advise of the happenings aboard another boat. Joe was instructed to verify that everyone was onboard.

Joe made his way to the owner's suites. He first knocked on Tomas' door twice until a response was received. "Just checking to see if you're awake, Sir?" he said then continued to Drake's cabin door to knock. He waited and after no response, he knocked again. "Drake, the captain asked for me to verify that everyone is onboard. Are you awake, Sir?" Joe called out but again, no response. He turned the knob and entered the empty room only to find the bed still made.

Uncertain if perhaps Drake was sharing a bed with his wife, Joe then proceeded to Melody's door and knocked. As he waited for a response, Tomas' door suddenly opened. Drake appeared seeming to be sleepy while fixing his hair and buttoning last night's shirt. He gave Joe a worried glance and said, "I was just checking on Tomas."

Joe immediately knew Drake's story. It was no secret that Melody and Drake had a loveless marriage. As a gay man himself, Joe always had his doubts about Drake in many ways. Drake proceeded to his room as Joe knocked again on Melody's door. "Mel are you awake? The captain asked that I make sure everyone is onboard and okay." he called out but still no answer. Joe entered the room and the only signs of occupancy were last night's clothes on the floor. Joe knocked and opened the door to the bathroom but it was empty.

Worried over Melody's whereabouts, Joe hurried to the bridge to advise the captain that Melody was missing. Together, they found Drake and Tomas and they all searched every inch of the boat but she was absent. The captain contacted the Coast Guard to advise.

The Coast Guard brought Drake to the other boat to identify the body. It was confirmed that the mystery woman in the water was indeed the famous Melody Bliss. It didn't take long for the news to spread globally. Melody's publicity photo was gracing the cover of newspapers around the world but was it an accident or a murder?

Everyone on the boat that evening was questioned more than once. Joe's disclosure about Drake coming out of Tomas' room raised lots of questions and eyebrows among the detectives. It was at a time when being openly gay would have been career suicide. Tomas and Drake both denied anything romantic, which was the truth. Their relationship was discreetly sexual but never intended as a romance.

Months passed with Drake fielding questions from attorneys, the press, the entertainment industry, friends and families. The official cause of death listed was an accidental drowning. However, the rumors surrounding Melody's death were ongoing and speculative. The most speculation and greatest rumors were too juicy and being spread by none other than Melody's greatest rival, Lydia Carlisle.

After a dramatic appearance at the funeral, Lydia made the rounds with the press. Under the premise of defending her "good friend's good name", Lydia did her best to dismiss the boring facts while fanning the fiery whispers of controversy. It was all to protect Melody's memory, or so Lydia said, but she had designs on a role.

Melody would have thrown herself off of that boat many times over if she had known that Lydia wanted to play her in a film. Shopping around the story to the studios seemed like a formality to Lydia. Her quest to get her hooks into a story that was at the forefront of the world's attention seemed like a must. Perhaps Melody's death was still too recent for a film. None of the studios would touch it.

Undaunted, Lydia backed the production with her own money. She gathered her favorite writers and director and became executive producer and star. Drake and Tomas protested what they described as inaccuracies in the story of Melody's life and death. Lydia simply used partial facts while fictionalizing her film, *"A Star is Mourned"*.

The film was released and fed off of the considerable publicity that had never dissipated over Melody's much publicized death. The public flocked to see the film assuming that its every detail was fact when it was not but that didn't matter to Lydia. As was the case for just about anything Lydia touched, it turned to gold…a gold statue.

When the nominations for the prestigious Marlon award were made the following year, Lydia's name was at the top of the list. The film was hailed as a triumph and, as usual, Lydia's performance a strong contender to win, which she did. Of course, in accepting her latest accolade, Lydia lauded Melody's talent and bemoaned her death.

Drake and Tomas carried on with their roles on their soap opera all the while keeping their secret safe from the night Melody died. The passage of time eventually took them decades past that fateful night aboard the *Blissful*. Neither would ever speak with the press again regarding Melody's untimely death or the circumstances involved.

Joe went on to work for other big-name Hollywood stars but it was his time working for Melody that opened doors. His observation of Drake leaving Tomas' room in the early hours that day left him believing there was more to Drake's story than he would admit. The authorities also had their doubts but nothing could ever be proven.

Drake eventually married another actress and together, they lived comfortably off of Melody's money. The presence of a second wife gave Drake a beard to use in dispelling those pesky and persistent rumors that he was gay. By way of Joe's speculation, Drake and Tomas would be forever linked as contributing to Melody's death.

Years later, the captain went to the police and the press claiming that he heard Melody and Drake arguing the night of her death. Previously, he had told the police that he heard nothing. It was after Drake came to him the morning of Melody's death that he was told that there was no argument and to say nothing. At that time, the captain felt uncertain as to what he heard. He also felt that Drake was seeming nervous but it was dismissed as anguish over the loss of his wife. Melody's fall versus a push forever remained a mystery.

Chapter 4

How the Mighty have Fallen

It was an orchestra of noises bellowing from the organized chaos on sound stage seventeen of a major studio on a hot 1990s July day. The lighting people were arguing with the electricians over the need for additional power to adequately light the set's exterior shots. The wardrobe department was getting annoyed with the director over yet another change with insufficient time to finish before filming.

The heat was oppressive from both the lighting and the season. Tempers flared, as did egos of the diva stars both male and female. Profanities flew between the male lead and the director over the next shot showing the star's right side versus his left. "My left is my best side. I want it shot from my left." the actor demanded in a snit.

The salty-mouthed director, who wasn't resetting the shot to show a dimple, explained "The ocean is on your right and you're talking to somebody on your left. You're going to talk to somebody with your back to them?" The actor wasn't giving-in, "Just reset the fucking shot." It would become a feud resolved by the executive producer.

Among the ranks of many busy workers was a young upstart to the industry named Erik Edelman. This theater junky from high school made every effort to break into the business. His best friend from drama class in Pittsburgh thought his good looks would open doors as an actor. Unfortunately, good looks were more than plentiful in Hollywood. Erik became lost in a sea of several other pretty faces.

When acting failed to pay the bills, this would-be star took the first job he could find at any studio. If he couldn't work as an actor, he could be surrounded by them while he did his best to break into the business. Today marked the beginning of only his second week on the job as a lowly assistant to the director doing just about anything.

"Kid, what's your name again?" the director asked from a cloud of smoke delivered by his ever-present cigarette. "Erik, Sir." he replied in his timid tone. "Look, Erik...I need you to take these script changes to the boss across the lot, Bungalow One. Got it?" the man said as he handed him a script. "Yes, Sir!" Erik replied and hurried away to find the man in charge who was working in Bungalow One.

Upon arrival at Bungalow One, Erik read the name on the door. "Harry Mond" sounded so made-up to Erik but, in Hollywood, most people changed their names, not just the actors. Most likely, Mond was short for something else. Erik liked the name. "Maybe I'll change my name." he thought to himself as he knocked on the door.

"Come in!" he heard a loud, masculine voice shout out. Turning the knob, Erik opened the door slowly as not to interrupt. Sitting at the largest desk he had ever seen, Erik saw a man leaning back in a wide, expensive-looking chair with his hands folded behind his head. He was looking up and making faint groaning sounds. "I'll be with you in a minute." he said as Erik stood clutching the script.

Erik waited as this man seemed to continue in a pensive state and breathing heavily. Erik thought is seemed odd that this man would be thinking so hard that he struggled to breathe. Suddenly, the man took both hands and clutched the arms of his chair, "Oh yeah, that's it...that's it...Oh, God!" he said in a breathy pant of ecstasy or pain.

"Whew! You better get back to your desk." Mr. Mond said in a tone of exhaustion. "I don't have a desk, Sir!" Erik replied. Suddenly, a woman crawled out from under his desk. Her breasts were exposed as she refastened her bra and brushed off her knees and tight skirt. Looking only mildly embarrassed, the woman left the room and returned to the outer office where she was apparently the secretary.

Erik stood wide-eyed at the obvious lack of discretion displayed by Mr. Mond's afternoon delight. Being a virgin from a conservative family, he had never participated in any kind of sexual activity. In fact, his knowledge of certain acts was limited to locker room tales from high school classmates who were probably just as unworldly.

Uncertain of what to say, Erik looked down at the floor as he told Mr. Mond why he was there, "Sir, the director on stage seventeen told me to bring these changes to you." he said as he walked toward the desk. The next sound Erik heard was that of a zipper from Mr. Mond's hands that were in his lap. Erik gently placed the script on the corner of the desk and asked, "Do you need anything else, Sir?"

Completely lacking in any sense of modesty or decorum, Mr. Mond replied, "Have a seat over there and I'll let you know when these are ready to go back to the director." Erik looked over to a lone chair placed in a corner. It almost seemed like something a parent would have placed for an unruly child to contemplate bad behavior.

Following orders, Erik sat in the chair thinking it would be only a few minutes before he would depart. One hour passed and the man hadn't even opened the script. He sat making and receiving phone calls, thumbing through papers and doing pretty much anything other than looking at the script. After nearly three hours, Mr. Mond tossed the untouched script in Erik's direction and said, "Tell the director that I approved his changes." Erik picked it up and left.

The entire visit to Bungalow One was the most bizarre event that had ever occurred in Erik's life. Between the live sex show and the multi-hour wait for no apparent reason, Erik was uncertain why he even had to make the journey. In Hollywood, executive producers were known to be tyrants. Most had little to no regard for others. All they knew was that when they wanted something, anything, it was the job of someone to provide it. People were used like props.

As production continued, it became a near daily event for Erik to carry the script down to Bungalow One and wait. Some days, it was a few minutes and others might be two or more hours. During these odd and unpleasant visits, Erik just sat in the corner hoping for a quick release from his servitude as he listened to boring phone calls.

Unbeknownst to Erik, these multi-hour waits provided subliminal lessons on how to be a producer. He was learning by observation how to negotiate contracts, how to control a conversation, how to get his way and how to mistreat women. He didn't know it at the time but all of this information, good and bad, would be used later.

One day, Erik arrived at Bungalow One to find a new face behind the secretary's desk; younger and prettier than the one before. Erik was handed a hundred-dollar bill and told to take Mr. Mond's car to be detailed. When he returned, the young woman was in tears.

Erik wanted to console her and offer assistance but he didn't want to pry. She seemed to be anxiously gathering her belongings for departure. He was curious over the cause of her distress but didn't want to pry. As she was leaving, he noticed something out of place.

Her blouse was torn at the chest and buttons missing. Her stockings were ripped. He had no idea what had happened as she left in a hurry. Mr. Mond's powerful presence did not lend itself to ask why his new secretary was leaving or what had happened. Erik returned Mr. Mond's keys and retrieved the script from him. It was the final day of filming and the last day that Erik ever visited Mr. Mond.

Time passed and Erik was quickly promoted as an assistant to a top producer, Wesley "Wes" Weinberg. He was a very tall man with the good looks of Hollywood leading men. In fact, he had been an actor in his earlier days but made a more successful transition behind the scenes in production. He was charming, polite and very well-liked.

It didn't take long before Erik found himself being schooled in the proper techniques of stroking artists' egos while minimalizing their compensation. It was the typical "carrot on a string", in that, if they would agree to take a little less now, something bigger was coming. After two years on the job, Erik was well-connected with agents, actors, producers and all of the trappings of a profitable industry.

Success had arrived for Erik in an unexpected form. He had his own office, a car, a nice home and more than enough money to enjoy. His working relationship with Wes thrived. Erik had met Wes' wife and children many times. Wes was a devoted family man. Erik had thrown himself into his new career. Romance was on hold.

One day, Erik was having difficulty getting an actress' agent to finalize a deal. She was making demands based on her client's last success. The studio needed her client and she knew it. Wes always had an open-door policy with Erik. He decided to visit Wes' office to seek his advice. Erik walked down the alley to Bungalow Six only to find Wes' secretary missing. Erik knocked, opened the door and found Wes' bare butt thrusting up and down on top of his secretary.

Hearing the door open, Wes was startled as he looked over to see Erik. "I'll be with you in a minute, Erik." he said in a relieved tone that it was only a friend who saw them. Erik closed the door quietly and waited until he could hear an obvious indication that Wes was satisfied. Minutes passed before his secretary made her exit smiling.

Days passed since Erik's untimely interruption of Wes' secretarial interlude. As was often the case, Erik was spending time with Wes and his family at their beach house. The kids were playing on the beach as their mother sat making sand castles while Wes waved.

"That's quite a family you've got there, Wes" Erik said as he and Wes sat on the deck overlooking his family. "Yeah, they're my pride and joy. They mean the world to me." Wes responded. Erik heard this claim knowing that just a few days earlier he found Wes having sex with his secretary. It seemed like hypocrisy to Erik. He felt that he knew Wes well enough to comment on marital obligation.

"Wes, can I ask you something?" Erik inquired. "Sure, anything." Wes replied. Erik seemed hesitant to ask but his curiosity reigned supreme. "Do you and your wife have an open relationship?" he asked as Wes gave a glower as if it was a bad joke. "No! Why would you ask such a question?" Wes asked with a tone of offense.

Not wanting to be rude but unwilling to sweep the matter under the rug with someone who was a friend, Erik explained, "You're having an affair with your secretary. Wouldn't your wife be upset?" Wes sat in silence over Erik's breaking of an unwritten rule among male Hollywood producers to turn a blind eye to their sexual escapades.

After a conspicuous pause, Wes offered some schooling to his friend and newbie colleague, "What affair? I got some on the side from my secretary. That's just one of the perks of the profession, man. You'll be getting some soon enough. Live it up. Everybody does it, man!"

Erik sat staring at Wes' toothy smile of an almost prideful display. It felt as if he was being ordered to have sex with women who were in a coerced situation of intimidation. The casting couch seemed dated.

Some men claimed these women consented because they thought it might further their career. Erik wondered how many were forced. Erik could not help but recall that poor woman leaving Mr. Mond's office that day in tears with ripped clothing. It lingered like a bad dream. Hearing Wes' claim that "Everybody does it!" offended him.

More time passed and Erik's career had grown into a position of authority. He had become one of a dozen powerful producers at the studio and they were all men. Not one woman could be found in any production position higher than assistant producer. It was a man's world and they held all the power to make or break someone.

The year was now 2017 and Erik had been in the industry for nearly twenty years with the latter half being as an executive producer. During those years, he had seen many an actress, crew member, secretary and female staff member come and go quickly. Some did not go quietly as they made claims of broken promises and sexual assault that were quickly and quietly settled by the studio bosses.

Also over the years, he had witnessed various sexual acts between other producers and their staff or cast. He had discussions with human resources and the legal department. However, he was told that there were no official complaints and that asking too many questions could lead to the end of his career. He was silenced as the bad press could have a devastating effect on a studio's reputation.

Erik knew there was a systemic failure in addressing the problem. He knew that for every woman who spoke up, there were probably many others who were afraid to say anything. Shame, fear and the intimidation of powerful men who could ruin them brought silence. Erik felt the need to do something but he worried about his career.

One day, there was a woman on the news standing next to her high-profile attorney. Her claims went beyond inappropriate touch by a Hollywood power broker of a producer. Her claim was rape and it was made against none other than Harry Mond. It, allegedly, had happened years earlier. She had gone to the studio bosses to complain but was told to stay silent or be sued for lack of evidence.

Erik carefully watched the press conference unfold. He realized that the woman in question was the same woman leaving Mr. Mond's office with torn clothing. "Oh my, God!" he whispered to himself. Of course, Mr. Mond denied any wrong doing and threatened legal action for defamation. When asked, "Why now?" the attorney gave the explanation that it took years to find proof of her claim of rape.

After the incident, Mr. Mond made the mistake of mentioning that he had to "Take an opportunity that didn't want to be taken." in an email to another producer. The other producer's secretary had full access to all of his emails. After the secretary declined advances, she felt her job was on the line so she searched for proof to make public. It turned out to be a situation of a little bad press goes a long way.

This network of powerful deviants was swept under the rug by the studios. It quickly unraveled as dozens of producers were exposed for the perverts they were. Once this first woman came forward, it was then a snowball effect of dozens of other women, and a few men, who now felt safe enough to share their stories of intimidation.

Among the names of the mighty who had fallen were Harry Mond and Wesley Weinberg. Big name actresses, unknowns and staff all came forward by the droves to start a movement of change not just for the film industry but for anyone's unwanted sexual advances.

After police investigations, evidence was sufficient enough to call for the arrest of some of the highest-ranking studio executives on the charge of rape. Some were hauled away from their homes and offices in handcuffs with the press anxiously waiting for a photo op.

In a matter of days, many of these power brokers lost their careers, their marriages, their money and worst of all, their clout. Spouses filed for divorce. Children were shamed for their parent's behavior. Studios were scrambling to do their best to provide damage control.

Not every high-profile producer was guilty of sexual impropriety, including Erik. However, they were all at risk of suspicion. That's when Erik volunteered to be the first to testify against the others.

Thinking that he was making appropriate efforts, Erik approached the powers that be at the highest ranks of studio authority. He made an offer to tell what he knew and what he saw over the years as a producer. The studio was publicly claiming to seek out facts and bring justice to any wrongdoing. Erik assumed he'd be welcomed. His assumption was proven wrong. The studio wanted his silence.

"You're not going to make things better by bringing in more details for us to investigate. We want this matter kept to a minimum." The CEO of the studio told him during a face-to-face meeting. Erik was shocked and uncertain as to how to proceed but he'd find a way.

Uncertain of his future now that he had made his himself known as a witness, Erik began searching through emails. He was weeding through hundreds of emails going back years looking for any signs of impropriety. Sexual references that he had previously ignored in his male-dominated workplace were now treasures to be found.

The email system only went back for thirty-six months. However, what was found was potentially enough. He wanted to force the studio to do more than disperse empty promises to an intolerant public and media. Mostly, he found brief but graphic references of certain aspects of women's bodies. The responses included other's cheering them on to "tap that ass" and "ask for some quid pro quo".

After hours of searching, Erik managed to find more than a handful of inappropriate comments. Not enough to convict someone for an assault but there were two; one from Harry and one from Wes that were sufficiently incriminating. Erik printed them out to save in case he needed something to protect his name and/or his job later.

The studio continued making minimal efforts. Wes, Harry and several others were fired. It brought their production teams to a halt as new producers were brought onboard. Mostly women who had previously and unsuccessfully tried to ascend to an executive level. One day, Erik was told to meet with the studio legal team. He was advised that his name had been linked to some impropriety and that he was being terminated. He knew it was all lies to silence him.

Erik was unwilling to allow these false accusations to be levied against him without a fight. They were a thinly-veiled attempt to discredit him and any allegations he might make. If he corroborated the claims of these women, the studio could be in a greater position of liability and they were trying to silence every possible witness.

It was irony wrapped in hypocrisy for a studio to publicly claim to be investigating while trying to stymie those who would speak up. Erik took his case to the same attorney who was representing the woman making the original claim of sexual assault. He presented his email evidence, which he was told would help to bring justice.

The list of plaintiffs seeking remuneration from the accused and the studio now included Erik's name. He sought damages for being defamed and for whistleblower retaliation. The legal battles were mounting and each week brought new victims coming forward. It reached a point that the court had to consolidate the lawsuits into a class action suit in order to expedite resolution. Progress was slow.

Finally, a trial was set and testimony began. One by one, accusers had their moment to tell their story. Of course, defense attorneys would claim these were consensual indiscretions. However, there was just enough proof to convince a jury that, at least, some of these acts were forced. Both of Erik's claims of whistleblower retaliation and defamation were thrown out, very much to everyone's surprise.

The studio was claiming that he was part of the problem because he knew of improprieties and said nothing when it happened. By his own admission, he saw a woman leaving Mr. Mond's office in tears with torn clothing and he did nothing to assist her. He didn't confront Mr. Mond, he didn't contact human resources or the top brass at the studio to advise of his observations. He did nothing.

Unlike his mentors and colleagues, Erik was basically a good guy. He never sexually harassed anyone. He never raped anyone. He never enticed an artist to consensually participate in a sexual act to further their career. He never did any of those things. However, he failed to help victims at the time he discovered their victimization.

Despite his best intentions after somebody else spoke up, his efforts were too little and too late. Complicity by negligence was his crime and it brought him the same loss of livelihood as those found guilty of rape and coercion. He tried going elsewhere but other studios wouldn't hire him because of his association with such a scandal.

In his mind, Erik was innocent of wrongdoing. However, in the eyes of the victims and the law, he might as well have held down these victims while crimes were being committed against them. Looking the other way while someone in power was having sex in their office with their secretary made him an inadvertent accomplice.

The notion that some people consented so it must have been alright silenced the voices of those who did not consent. Hollywood was a tough town in which to succeed but the privilege of power was not above the law. People were behaving badly just because they could.

It took time but, eventually, Erik saw the error of his ways. He lost everything for which he had accomplished but it had a silver lining. His modest standard of living coupled with his profitable, multi-decade career afforded him the ability to form his own production company. His first endeavor was to produce a documentary on the very scandal in which he became entangled. It was his redemption.

The film was a tedious project of arduous interviews. Much to his surprise, two people willing to be interviewed were Harry and Wes. Harry was serving time for rape and both he and Wes had already lost everything. They had nothing more to lose by speaking with Erik and his crew. In fact, it became their chance to apologize.

Erik's film had a limited release but the viewership was substantial enough to make it a success. He chose to donate his proceeds to establish a victim's fund. The reviews were favorable enough to garner a nomination of the highest award. The night arrived for the awards show. Erik and his team were hopeful for a win. He wanted a chance to explain the film's origin and to apologize for his part. He was elated when he heard the presenter confirm his redemption, "And the winner is, Erik Edelman for *How the mighty have fallen.*"

Chapter 5

My Mother, My Wife

It was an endless bottleneck of rush hour traffic causing the late arrival to an important audition of struggling actress, Rose Barlow. For what was hopefully the last time, a glance at her watch brought an impatient sigh. "Driver, can you please hurry. I'm going to miss my audition." she said in a snippy tone as the man stared back at her in the rearview mirror and replied, "Lady, I'm doing my best!"

Upon arrival curbside in front of the studio gates, Rose gave a brief glance to the meter. Taxi fares of the late 1940s being what they were, the two dollars and change owed were more than covered by the five-dollar bill that Rose handed the driver. Urgency to her appointment had her forego a wait for change, "Keep it!" she said as she hurried from the car, closed the door and ran to the guard.

After verification of her appointment, the guard directed her to the back-lot office of the famous director, Ray Nichols. She hurried as much as her high heels and tight skirt would allow. Seeing the office door with Mr. Nichols' name on it, she yanked it open while being out of breath from her sprint. Greeting Rose was a stern looking older woman peering at her through nose perched glasses.

"Name?" the stony-faced secretary asked without any salutation or interest. Rose stood with her hand to her chest trying to catch her breath. "Rose...Rose Barlow" she said with a forced pant of each syllable. The woman gave a look of disapproval and replied, "I'm sorry Miss Barlow but you're late. I'll have to call you if Mr. Nichols decides to reschedule." Rose sighed in disappointment but refused to surrender to finality without one more attempt at being seen.

"Oh, please, ma'am! I know I'm late but traffic was awful. If you could please just let Mr. Nichols know that I'm here now..." Rose pleaded until disinterest caused an interruption by the secretary, "I'm sorry, Miss Barlow." Just then, the door to the director's office opened and a young woman exited with a smile to a handsome gentleman who bid her farewell. Rose seized the opportunity, "Mr. Nichols, I'm Rose Barlow and I'm so sorry that I'm late." she said. Mr. Nichols admired her stunning beauty. "Welcome Miss Barlow!" he said as he led Rose past his secretary's glower of doom.

Once in his office, the director handed Rose a script and offered a brief explanation of the scene and the character's motivation. He listened to her delivery and was intrigued but he needed it to be read another way, "Could you please try it again with an almost tearful plea? Pretend you're trying to get past my secretary." he said with a chuckle as Rose gave a slight smile. "Yes, Sir!" she replied.

He watched her performance and despite the fact that it seemed a little forced in its delivery, he could see her obvious raw talent. They sat for nearly an hour discussing the role and his vision for the film's final result. Rose offered her opinion on a few of his points and together, they seemed to have an obvious rapport. It would lend itself well to her playing the role for which she had auditioned.

"How about some lunch and we can discuss this further?" he said with a charming smile as he stood from his masterful perch behind his desk. Rose smiled at the invitation as she stood and asked, "Does this mean that I have the role?" Mr. Nichols slipped on his jacket and replied, "I can't think of anyone better to play the role of Gloria, Miss Barlow." Rose's joy over her anxiously anticipated big break was obvious, "Oh, thank you Mr. Nichols!" she said happily. "There is just one requirement. You must call me Ray and I'll call you Rose" he said sweetly as he led her to the door. She smiled in affirmation and gave his secretary a victorious smirk as they left.

Weeks went by and the film was now fully cast and well into its production. Sets had been built, costumes had been made and Rose had learned her lines in painstaking detail. Her role as Gloria was that of the unfaithful housewife of a best-selling author whose sudden fame causes him to neglect his wife. Gloria gets involved with a married man who abandons his wife and family for her.

Eventually, the characters marry and meet their demise through a tragic accident. The role of Gloria is a small role with barely nine minutes of screen time. However, Rose's performance is compelling enough to bring her a nomination for the film industry's top award. Despite the brevity of her role and it being her first film, Rose wins the award. Her life is forever changed thanks to her director, Ray.

After the onset of her unexpected fame, Rose finds herself receiving numerous offers for other films. She had her pick of any number of scripts with her choice of directors. After careful consideration and consultation with Ray, Rose opts for another drama and another chance to work with the man who gave to her career a trajectory of success. By the time that contracts were signed, Rose and Ray had more than a working relationship. Their lives were imitating that of the role of Gloria. Ray was a married man with a young son and a loving wife but it wasn't enough. Ray and Rose were now in love.

One thing that was different between Ray and Gloria's love interest in his previous film was that Ray would never leave his son. He gave just enough money to his now ex-wife that, despite infidelity, permitted him to retain his parental rights. Eventually, Rose and Ray were married and, at times, Ray's young son, Tony, would stay a few days or weeks with his father. It was important to Ray that Rose and Tony not have any animosity as child and step-parent.

Rose did her best to seek Tony's love and respect. She welcomed him into their home with unconditional love of a parent. Every holiday and birthday were honored with a celebration appropriate for the child of someone who was now a successful movie star.

Driven by the hormones of an early teen, Tony's love for his step-mother had morphed into something that was inappropriate. At times, when his father was not home, Tony would sometimes sneak into the master bedroom while Rose while grooming and dressing. In what he considered to be luck, during these covert escapades of indecency, Tony often played voyeur by watching Rose shower.

As time passed, Rose felt the onset of Tony's crush on her. He was becoming a young man who was no longer the young child she had first met. Eventually, Tony told his mother that he wanted to go live with his father. Despite her apprehension over her son living full-time with his father and his once mistress, Tony's mother consented to his request. Tony was now at home with Rose daily if she was between making films. Ray was frequently gone on set with his latest films. Rose and Ray's love would soon see a severe waning.

Eventually, Ray's schedule became more and more demanding as his reputation for award winning direction began to flourish. Rose's film offers continued but, over time, the number of good scripts began to diminish until they became more infrequent. Rose was getting lonely and bored at home day after day, week after week waiting for her husband to come home. Some nights, he never made it home while claiming production delays and sleeping in his office.

The demands of Ray's thriving career left Tony and Rose at home with greater frequency. By the time that Tony was in his mid-teens, Rose was starting to question if Ray was having an affair. Afterall, if he had an affair with Rose while married to his first wife, what was to stop him from having an affair while married to his second wife?

More time passed and Rose's accusations to Ray about his infidelity were soon becoming harder and harder to deny. He would come home very late with lipstick residue on his lips. Apparently, his efforts to wipe off the evidence was minimal. He frequently had an aroma of perfume. Ray had an explanation for every claim of his wife's suspicions but, eventually, Rose felt no love or trust in Ray.

One day, while home alone with Tony, Rose was returning some clothing that the maid had mixed in with his father's. Making her way down the hall to Tony's room, Rose found the door slightly ajar as she knocked and entered the room. "Tony, I have some of your clothes." she said uncertain if he was in the room. She looked over to find the door to his bathroom open wide and him in the shower.

Still in his teens but old enough to drive or join the military, Tony was clearly no longer a little boy in the physical aspect. Rose was taken by surprise at his nudity in the shower. He very much had a man's physique. In addition, he was masturbating in the shower. She knew that she should have left the room immediately but her carnal instincts reigned supreme despite their history. She couldn't stop watching him attending to natural urges until he was satisfied. As she heard the water being turned off, she left the clothes on his bed and hurried out of the room. As Tony reached for his towel, he was certain that he saw Rose leaving the room. He closed the door.

The incident of Rose's voyeurism into Tony's shower played out over and over again in her mind. It bothered her because he was her step-son. It seemed so inappropriate but simultaneously so alluring. She knew that if he had been her biological child, she never would have these urges but he wasn't. It was a fact that he was somebody else's child. Tony was unsure if Rose saw him in the shower but he also didn't mind the possibility that she had. They both had urges.

More time passed and Ray was finishing production on his latest film. Rose was in constant complaint over his being absent so much. Ray decided to hurry home to announce that he was taking time off before his next film in order to spend time with his wife and son. He assumed that would make Rose happy enough to try to rekindle the love that was slowly and noticeably slipping away from them both.

Ray pulled up to their house late into the evening, tired and hungry. He entered the house through the kitchen and decided to search through the refrigerator for nourishment before heading to bed. He assumed that Rose was asleep. He'd wake her up for a late-night romp followed by a little pillow talk to announce his time off.

After finishing his meal and attending to the dog who was in need of last-minute visit outside, Ray entered their bedroom and quietly made his way to the bathroom to shower and brush his teeth. Dried off but still wrapped in a towel, he made his way over to their bed where he dropped the towel on the floor and reached over to wake Rose. He felt around and discovered that Rose was not in the bed.

He turned on the light and found her side of the bed still made. He walked to the door of the hallway, slipped on his robe and began to search for Rose. She was nowhere to be found. He had seen her car in the garage so she had to be home. Suddenly, there was a slight noise that sounded like a giggle. He continued down the hallway until he got to the last room, which was Tony's. He listened through the door and heard the sound of a woman's voice. His son was barely eighteen. He wouldn't permit him to bring a woman into the house for sex. Ray opened the door, turned-on the light and found Rose bare chested and straddling his son's nearly naked body.

Wide-eyed in shock, Ray was speechless as Rose and Tony looked panicked. Rose slid her nightgown back up over her breasts as she stepped onto the floor. Tony pulled up his underwear to cover his obviously aroused state. Ray couldn't believe what he was seeing.

"I'm not even going to ask what going on because that's obvious. What I'll never understand is why." Ray said to his wife and to his son before looking to Rose and continuing, "You have five minutes to pack a bag and get out of this house or I'm calling the police." He then turned to Tony and said, "You can go live with your mother, go in the military, I don't care but you can't live under my roof and fuck my wife. I want you both out of here NOW!" he screamed.

Tony and Rose said nothing as they gathered what belongings they each could fit into a single suitcase and left in their individual cars. Neither one ever spoke a word to apologize for their staggeringly inappropriate betrayals. After their departure, Ray sat quietly alone at the kitchen table with only a bottle of scotch to console him.

Rose camped out at a hotel for a few days until she heard from her attorney that Ray had filed for divorce. Neither Ray nor Rose would want the prying eyes of the press to publicize the humiliating cause of their split. Not wanting a long, drawn-out public disclosure, Ray agreed to let Rose have their house and a modest sum of money in lieu of alimony that was standard for women to receive at that time.

Ray threw himself into his work and took on as many projects as he could handle. Rose had only worked on a minimal basis since her big win of a prestigious award. She would now have to seek out new projects but her conspicuous absence from the limelight made it difficult to find work. In need of money, Rose took on a couple of low-budget films. After those flopped, she would turn to the stage.

Two years had passed since Rose and Ray divorced. Rose met a television producer who wanted her to star in his shows. Both using the other to further their careers, they quickly married and had a daughter. It didn't take long before their lack of compatibility overshadowed their whirlwind romance and they decided to divorce.

Two divorces were now behind Rose and motherhood of a young child ahead of her. Her second husband's modest success did not provide for a substantial divorce settlement. Meager child support and almost no alimony had her still struggling to pay the bills. The need for money had her seeking any work possible; a commercial, a soap opera, any film or television show either as the lead or even cameo appearances. Anything to keep her name in the public eye.

Staying busy while raising her daughter alone, Rose crossed paths with various actors. One such newcomer was her former step-son and lover, Tony Nichols. Tony had always held an interest in acting since his father was a director. Tony once tried to audition for his father but the audition was called off by Ray's stony-faced secretary.

Despite the humiliating circumstances of their previous liaison, Rose and Tony felt a deep attraction. Maybe it was lust or perhaps it was love but whatever the motivation, they soon found themselves dating. Despite their age difference, they eventually transitioned from step-parent and step-child to man and wife. When her second husband learned of her marriage to her former step-son, he filed for and was quickly awarded sole custody of their young daughter.

Tony and Rose ignored the press and the controversy to continue on with their marriage. They eventually had two sons together. For the most part, they were happy but as the years past, the age difference became a bigger issue for Tony. After fourteen years, they divorced.

Now in her fifties with three divorces and three children, Rose was feeling the icy touch of fate's cruel destiny. After years of a hard life, Rose's beauty was noticeably fading. Hollywood was not known for being a place where aging gracefully was embraced and Rose felt it.

She turned to plastic surgery to retain her disappearing youth but limited means would not afford her the best surgeons available. The result was a look about her of an older woman desperately trying to look younger. In her mind, it was money well-spent and nobody noticed the obvious. To the Hollywood press, producers and her waning public, Rose Barlow was becoming a cocktail party joke.

The scandalous marriage to her first husband's son and her now altered face brought pity and ridicule. The press and public were unkind while Rose did what she could to salvage her career. By the time her children were grown, her career was minimal at best. Her image of herself was completely out of sync with Hollywood's.

It was a bitter dose of reality to see just how easily one can go from accomplished actor to notable has-been. Her previous award could get her an audition but her lack of recent success often prevented her from getting the job. Still, she had just enough of a name that, in certain places, she could still earn a living. Mostly, it was overseas.

As was the case for many Hollywood stars, fame seemed to prevail over infamy in other countries. Rose was no exception, in that, her previous films were well known and revered. Despite her surgical efforts, she could still get recognized and asked for autographs in other countries. England was especially fond of her previous films.

Searching for opportunity in any form, Rose hired a London talent agent to find work for her in the theater or films. There were a few roles significant enough for her to earn a decent living while maintaining her celebrity status. She did a few plays and at every performance, autograph seekers waited for her at the stage door.

Perhaps it was the stoic, mid-century English sense of decorum that prevented snide comments about Tony. Rose didn't question her good standing with the public in England. She did her job as an actress and entertainer and was grateful for the work and notoriety.

The years rolled by rather quickly. Rose had been enjoying her new life in the more urbane surroundings of a continental audience. As is the case for anyone growing older, her mind and memory were starting to slip a little. At times, she would forget lines while on the stage. All actors were guilty of slip-ups but hers were escalating.

At the end of a long run of a popular play in London's West End, Rose was having minor bouts of disorientation. At times, she got scenes from plays confused with her real life and become agitated.

After her poor performances during her final few weeks in London, the producers of the play were not interested in using her again. Word among production companies quickly spread that Rose was struggling to deliver the performances for which audiences paid. It was a difficult dose of reality sending Rose into a major depression.

Hollywood had not sent her a script in years and now her star had faded over the London theatre district. Rose's options were now limited to whatever personal appearances her agent could plead for her to receive. There were a few low paying television commercials and media ads. There was the "chat show" circuit that paid scale.

It wasn't much of an existence but when television audiences heard her rambling rants, it wasn't hard to find her lost in confusion. At the suggestion of her agent, Rose returned to Hollywood to seek medical attention. Her children came to her rescue in helping to get her life organized and her medical care arranged for evaluation.

After more than one consultation, doctors were in disagreement as to the cause of her mental decline. One said she was suffering from severe depression over the loss of her career. Another said that she was suffering from a nervous breakdown for similar reasons. Both had suggested electroshock therapy after medications failed to help.

Against the better judgement of her daughter, Rose was taken by her sons to receive a series of electroshock treatments. Their hope and that of her physicians was that the treatments would help to calm her. The treatments were intended to help her adjust to the fact that she was growing older and at the end of her once stellar career.

Over the course of a few weeks, Rose had a small number of these treatments. They left her in a temporary state of confusion but rather serene after a few hours of haze. It helped her deal with her fame fading into a faint memory that was part of Hollywood life.

Rose made peace with her life as an ordinary person who used to be a famous star. Her first two husbands had passed away but, at her sons' request, Tony came to see her for what would be the last time.

Upon arrival, Rose was almost unrecognizable. Their age difference was very obvious at this point as she seemed like a very old lady to him. Rose was so faded from her feeble mind that she really didn't remember Tony until their sons reminded her of their marriage.

"Oh, of course. How have you been?" she asked in an insincere tone. Together, Tony and Rose sat for a few minutes talking about old times that she didn't remember until it was time for him to say his goodbye. "He seems like a nice man." She said to her eldest son.

Rose's final years were spent first in the care of her children and later in that of a nursing facility. It was a difficult decision for her family to place her into the care of strangers but Rose's mind was so far gone that she could no longer remember her children's names.

One day, while sitting in the common area of the nursing home, a movie was being shown on television. It was the film for which Rose had won her famous award. It was a small group of elderly souls who were unknowingly seated with one of the stars from the film. Rose watched intensely as if she was watching an old home movie. It sparked a brief moment of lucidity as she leaned in closer.

That face was an intangible memento. "Who is she? She looks so familiar." she said as the others sat in silence unable to answer her question. Rose reached over to the television screen and touched it while her character was speaking. "Oh my, God. It's me!" she cried. The other residents began to complain of her blocking the screen. That one moment of that fateful day watching her film on television would be her last time seeing any reminder of her long-lost career.

Rose was later diagnosed with breast cancer. Due to her advanced age and diminished mental state, her children opted to forego the usual treatments to prolong her life. It would seem to be a cruel attempt at delaying the inevitable. Rose had not always proven to be a good wife but she was always a kind mother doing her best for her children. They wanted to reciprocate. Rose Barlow lived out her final days surrounded by those who loved her unconditionally. Hollywood lost a talented star with an unseemly but forgiven past.

Chapter 6

Lights, Camera, Action

Distinct erotic moans could be heard from the apartment next door from that of a once famous television actor named Todd Maine. It was assumed by his neighbors that he was "at it again" but to what extent, they would never know. The fall of a 1960s sitcom star had hit its low point. Todd had to take shelter in the low-rent district of Hollywood in a shabby chic motif apartment with paper-thin walls.

On the other side of that wall was a den of iniquity complete with video equipment. Todd's latest covert production included a young, unsuspecting co-star whom he had met in a bar earlier that day. She was a desperate soul who fell prey to the circumstances of survival. For the mere price of a few dollars, she was Todd's brief sex prop.

As his naked backside thrust up and down on top of her body, he periodically looked up at the camera concealed between a stack of books. He smiled for personal pleasure and posterity during what would become his post production review of his latest performance. The woman under him had no idea of, nor interest in, his celebrity.

Todd finished his living room sexcapade in the usual manner in which these acts end. He tossed the condom in the direction of a desk-side trash can but it missed. It didn't matter. The clutter that was the trashy décor of his humble abode overshadowed the miss.

"You were great!" he said to the young woman who was anxiously dressing. Todd handed her the money he promised and she made a swift departure as he slipped on his underwear. His friend, Henry, entered the room from the usual hiding spot of the only bedroom. It was a furtive routine of two deviantes obsessed with amateur porn.

"Play it back. I want to see how I looked when I came." Todd said to his willing accomplice. Following orders, as he always did, Henry hurried to the controls of their concealed camcorder to fulfill Todd's request. "I don't know. I really don't look like I'm enjoying it." he said to Henry who was pretending to study the footage. "I think you look okay. She seemed to like it." Henry replied in a reassuring tone. Todd rewound the tape over and over again while critiquing. "My ass looks good. Look how it clinches when I cum." Todd said.

Todd's activities satisfied his present-day need to be in front of the camera after his once popular family sitcom ended years ago. Previously known as "America's Dad", he was nothing like the character that made him famous. Unfortunately, his show ran well before sitcom salaries and residuals were the huge payouts of today.

He was a struggling actor prior to his success and he returned to the same socio-economic status after the show ended. In fact, what he struggled with the most after he was unemployed was the loss of notoriety. During the show's heyday, he would be mobbed at just about any location. Now, time passed brought a return to obscurity.

Heavy drinking and hard living had aged this once good-looking heartthrob to the point that not even his neighbors recognized him. If they had, they'd probably be appalled to know that the father they watched on television as kids was now making amateur porn.

Adding to Todd's spiraling existence was his so-called friend, Henry. He was what most would describe as a mooch and a good-for-nothing parasite that needed a place to stay. Todd and Henry were introduced by one of Todd's former co-stars after that co-star was hoping to get Henry to stop pestering him. It was a disservice.

At the height of his career, Todd needed an assistant. Someone to handle the fans, their mail, requests for autographed photos and to do his personal errands. Henry was an obsessive groupie who penetrated the studio's lack of security between the stars and their fans. Henry got a job on the lot. It gave him access to all of the stars.

After Todd's show ended; after he had to sell his house to survive; after he sold his expensive car and drained most of his savings; Henry was still there wanting to be part of a celebrity's world in any capacity. It was a sad existence with no place else to go for Henry.

Even after Todd could no longer pay him a salary, Henry still lingered. He slept on Todd's couch in exchange for being at Todd's beck and call. Get groceries, get the mail, get some girls, whatever Todd wanted, Henry managed to meet the needs of his faux "boss".

Todd's obsession with nudity and eventual sex addiction started at an early age. In his earliest years, he lingered around locker rooms for just a little too long. Staring at the men and how their bodies differed from his became a pass-time. When Todd entered his late teens, the locker room at school brought a fondness for voyeurism and exhibitionism. He liked to look at others and to be seen naked.

It was in his last year of high school that Todd's first semi-sexual experience occurred one day after school. Todd was on the football team and it was his job to gather all of the equipment as the other boys showered and left for the day. The coach was an older man with an ultra-macho persona that made being nude in front of each other no big deal. Just the guys ignoring each other's nakedness.

One day, Todd was running late in putting away the equipment. The coach must have thought everyone was gone for the day. Todd entered the locker room to shower and found the coach in the communal shower with his back to him. It wasn't difficult for Todd to realize that the coach was taking a long time to wash. When Todd turned on the water at the opposite end of the room, the coach was startled. He turned to look and in doing so displayed a full erection.

Perhaps embarrassed, or perhaps not, the coach turned his back to Todd but continued with his shower. Todd was taken by surprise of the situation and despite the fact that he had never been attracted to men, he was aroused by the erotic nature of their shared space. Out of the corner of his eye, he watched the coach who glanced back. Eventually, Todd found himself unable to stop his body's reaction.

Before the two of them left the shower, they were facing each other in full display of the obvious acts of pleasuring themselves. At the end of this unexpected first experience with another person, there was no direct contact but it was mutually satisfying. Todd was not attracted to the coach but they did share a few more showers later.

Todd's early days of he and the coach giving each other an erotic show came to an abrupt end. The custodian happened to catch a matinee and the coach was soon fired for inappropriate behavior.

The lingering effects of Todd's high school escapades delivered to him a desire to continue with the intrigue of watching and being watched. The result was a life-long obsession with pornography. It first seemed a harmless situation of using magazines to gratify and satisfy natural urges. Later, it was frequent visits to seedy cinemas.

Even in Todd's younger days as a married man, his sexual fantasies were usually unfulfilled by the limitations of a conservative wife. He became guilty of what so many married men do, which was to satisfy his lust by using outside opportunities. Usually, these were less-than-legitimate massage parlors where a few extra dollars got you some extra relief. Over time, these occurrences had escalated. It took an STD exposure for Todd's wife to put an end to his infidelity.

Once Todd was a divorced man, unbridled opportunity was on the horizon. However, it was shortly after his divorce that he landed his big break in acting. He was now on television every week. That made for an impossible situation of him being able to visit adult bookstores and X-rated movies without being recognized by others.

Todd's obsession would have to go underground to more covert efforts. The money of his show's success afforded him equipment of a nearly professional caliber. Lighting was learned by the pros on set. Camera techniques were learned under the premise of his interest in how the show was made. His set soon became his school.

By the time that his show was in its third season, Todd became a master at staging equipment and lighting for his own productions. Unable to appear on camera himself, his faithful flunky Henry was a production assistant procuring low paid actors in these sex films.

Donning a minimal but sufficient disguise as not to be recognized, Todd became the director of these low-budget skin flicks. Together, Todd and Henry sold their inventory to various adult distribution companies. Discreetly disguised, Todd would frequently visit these back-alley theaters to catch a glimpse of his own work. He enjoyed watching other men pleasuring themselves to his films. If only these men knew who was behind the scenes of these raunchy romps.

Todd did have one close call in being recognized during what he called "auditions". In the middle of sweaty fury attempting to test his actress' skills, his fake beard fell off. Not missing a beat, Henry yelled "cut", threw Todd a towel to cover his face and said, "You've got the job, Honey. Be here tomorrow at two." She stared curiously.

At the height of popularity of Todd's weekly family program, he had become one of the leading producers of adult films. Henry was working around the clock arranging "actors" for their corny scripts. Todd may have been talented at staging and filming but writing was not his forte. It didn't matter as storyline was not the objective.

Henry's confidence as Todd's business partner had him wanting to branch out and try producing other films. The suggestion was made to consider producing gay porn as it was becoming more and more lucrative, according to Henry's research. Todd was not interested in watching two men have sex but he was interested in new revenue.

It was through Henry's persistence that they made a few gay films to see if they would sell. Afterall, "money is money" as Henry put it. Henry even offered to be the cameraman so that Todd wouldn't have to be present but Todd wanted his say in production quality.

Todd failed to realize that Henry never had a girlfriend or wanted to audition any of the women in their films. He wanted to be behind the scenes, until now. When men started answering their ads for all-male films, they had to be auditioned. Todd suggested having men audition with each other but Henry did his own private auditions.

Once their production company had a small stock of gay films in their inventory, distribution was attempted but the demand was minimal. Much to Henry's disappointment, Todd decided to cease production of that genre but Henry continued on behind his back.

The final season of Todd's show was coming to an end. As an actor, he would continue to seek new opportunities but he had been type-cast as the father figure. He wanted darker roles with grittier scripts but the best he could do was another sitcom that failed miserably.

Todd suffered significant financial setbacks after the demise of his hefty paychecks. Limited income, alimony, child support to his five children and personal expenses left him broke. First, he sold his house, then his expensive car was replaced by a beat-up klunker. Next, his investments that financial advisors promised him would payoff did not. He couldn't find an acting job. His stint on a sitcom closed more doors than it opened. Success left faster than it arrived.

Todd was living off of what was left of his savings while trying to survive day-to-day. His only income came in the form of a meager monthly residual check that was going away in a couple of years and his modest income from the porn that he and Henry produced. Eventually, he managed to get a few voiceover jobs working on cartoons and an occasional cameo role on various other shows.

Adding to his financial woes was Henry. He wanted to be cut in on the porn profits since Todd could no longer pay him a salary. It was Henry's first demand for money. Todd wanted to be fair since he needed Henry's help to make these films happen. He agreed to split the profits fifty-fifty with emphasis was on the word "profits". It was very easy to fake a loss based on exaggerated production costs.

Survival was Todd's first priority, not Henry. It wouldn't take long before betrayal between two disreputable business types surfaced. Henry was selling gay films under the table after he was told to stop making them. Todd was inflating costs to minimize shared profits. Both worked diligently to hide their dishonesty of hidden revenues.

In an effort to restart his career, Todd had fired his agent after he recalled a barracuda of an agent, Ruth Logan. Ruth had a reputation for persistence in getting her clients work and top-dollar for it. It was hard to get her as an agent but she had pursued Todd back when he first started his sitcom. She now agreed to represent him.

Ruth's first accomplishment was securing Todd a semi-reoccurring role on a weekly drama. She also promised to get him a deal for a new show within a year and she didn't make empty promises. For Todd, it felt as if his stalled career might be getting back on track.

Time passed and when he wasn't at the studio working on his new role, Todd was working with Henry in making new films. With the promise of a new series coming his way, he was wanting to make a quiet exit from the porn industry. Afterall, nothing would ruin his second chance faster than being exposed as a porn producer.

Periodically, Todd met with Ruth to share updates on his current role and her progress with lining up a new show. At times, Henry would be in-tow at these meetings as Todd's assistant. Ruth was a tough player in the entertainment industry. She didn't like it when stars, or their assistants, made demands of her as Henry tried to do.

Animosity was immediate between Todd's well-qualified agent and his unaccomplished assistant who was attempting to make a name for himself. At their first meeting, Henry tried to grill Ruth on the specifics of what she was doing and her progress. Ruth did not like nor would she accept some unknown lackey questioning her ability. She made it clear to Henry that Todd was her client, not him. Henry didn't like being put in his place when he was just trying to help.

Todd did his best to curb Henry's well-intended efforts because he had every bit of faith in Ruth. He didn't want his new agent getting frustrated and walking away. She was his ticket out of the depths of poverty, obscurity and porn. He desperately wanted to succeed.

Todd wanted to prepare Henry for his inevitable departure from the porn business. He decided to have a discussion about how to make that transition. While at lunch, Todd decided to bring-up the topic for an initial discussion to hear Henry's suggestions. He assumed that Henry would not mind being his own boss by making films.

While sipping margaritas at their favorite Mexican restaurant, Todd let alcohol set a mellow tone for discussion. "I want to talk to you about our film business. You know that once Ruth gets me a new contract that I won't be able to be involved with these films." Todd said to Henry who was sipping on the salty rim of a large beverage. "Why not? You were doing them with your last show." Henry said. Todd was trying to be polite but insistent, "Because I need out!"

Surprised that Henry was questioning his decision, Todd continued, "I like watching these films. I even like the perks of making them but I don't want it to be my life. I'm an accomplished actor. I don't want to throw my career away." His explanation for why the last few years' dark efforts were about to cease seemed to be falling flat.

Henry was staring back at Todd's beleaguered face as if he had the upper hand in his friend's decision to continue making films. "Well, I don't know what to say about this news. How am I supposed to survive? Am I going to give up making films to work for you?" he asked of a befuddled Todd who replied, "No, that wasn't my plan."

Henry seemed to become agitated to the point that alcohol was not soothing his ruffled feathers. He leaned closer to Todd and said in a whispered tone as not to have others hear, "Well, for years now, I've done everything for you. I've fetched your condoms, your toilet paper, your food and your films. I don't even get paid. My payment is sleeping on that dusty sofa bed of yours and crumbs off the table making cheap skin flicks with America's Dad. Big fucking deal!"

The relationship that had always been one of presumed boss and assistant had now taken a sharp, unexpected turn. Todd was taken by surprise at a side of Henry that he had never seen before. It was aggressive, possessive and demanding. He was uncertain if he was intimidated or impressed but he knew that he had to push back.

"Where's this attitude coming from? You haven't even heard my suggestion for how you benefit from this change. You wanna hear me out or do you just want to try to talk tough and piss me off?" Todd said with a grimace and his best effort to play the tough guy. Holding up his hands in a mock gesture of surrender, Henry replied "Sorry! I'm listening." Todd gave a look as if to say, "That's better!"

Pausing for the arrival of their food, Todd continued, "Once I have a new contract, you take over the entire production. You call the shots. You keep the inventory and keep all the revenue. I'll sell you the equipment and we wish each other well. I think that's pretty fair." Henry was silent as he pondered the details of Todd's plan.

Todd sat enjoying his food thinking that Henry would agree that paying him for the equipment was a fair buyout. His assumption would be incorrect. "Why should I pay you for the equipment if we both own the business? Isn't that equipment half mine?" Henry said in a defensive tone. Todd was surprised by Henry's terse rebuke.

"Look, I paid over thirty-grand for that equipment less than three years ago and you paid nothing. I'll sell it to you for half and you can even pay it out of your share of the profits between now and the time I get my new contract." Todd insisted. Henry was no longer distracted by his cocktail. His anger was mounting. The impending loss of his only link to a Hollywood celebrity and the suggestion that he should forfeit his only income for months seemed unfair.

"Oh, I paid nothing? I've paid my share and then some! I paid by being your bitch every day. You should be paying me for all of the work that I've done for you for free. How about if I just tell the world about your sex life for the past few years? What's that worth? I'm sure the tabloids would pay for some new equipment." Henry said in a seething tone as Todd's anger was beginning to boil over.

"Okay, we're done. I'm done with lunch and I'm done with you. Don't you ever threaten me again! I'll fucking kill you before I'll let you destroy my career. You're just some worthless leech. Find a new place to live and I'll just keep my equipment." Todd said as he stood and threw down some money, "I'll even pay for lunch, bitch!"

Todd stormed off playing the tough guy while feeling vulnerable to Henry's threats. He felt he knew Henry well enough to believe that he'd calm down and apologize later. Henry had always been very loyal to Todd who wanted to believe that these threats were idle anger. He held onto doubt that Henry would do anything rash.

Weeks passed and Todd had not heard from Henry. There was no indication that Henry was trying to sabotage his career. Ruth had made good on her promise to get Todd a new show. She decided to surprise Todd in person with the news and the actual contracts to sign. In a pre-GPS era, she followed a map to the address on file.

Upon arrival, Ruth was uncertain if she was at the correct address. The neighborhood seemed beyond poverty stricken. It seemed dangerous but she was tough enough to knock on the door. What she found was a door that was partially open. "Todd!" she called out as she pushed open the door while cautiously peeking inside.

"Todd, it's Ruth. I have some good news for you." She said as she looked around to see a pile of debris and electronic cords strewn about. Just then, she looked down and saw someone face down on the floor. She could see a large pool of blood surrounding the body. She ran to her car and drove to a pay phone to call for the police.

The news of Todd's murder spread quickly among the media. His former co-stars offered their condolences to his family. Henry was nowhere to be found. After interviewing friends, neighbors and Ruth, Henry was eventually tracked down for questioning. Having lived in the apartment, Henry's fingerprints were in replete supply.

What was also found were various adult films including some early day eight millimeters that starred none other than America's Dad. It was a scandal that Todd would have preferred to avoid for the sake of his children. What was conveniently not found was any of the equipment used by Todd and Henry to supply their porn business.

After considerable questioning, it was assumed that Henry had committed Todd's murder. There were no other suspects. The police felt the evidence was sufficient enough to charge Henry. The trial was a media sensation. It gave to Henry infamy in the absence of fame. The jury felt the evidence was insufficient to convict Henry. In the end, nobody else was ever charged with Todd Maine's murder.

Years rolled by and Henry was forever denying Todd's murder. He struggled with finding work because of his infamous past. Nobody, other than Todd and Henry, ever really knew the true nature of their relationship. The dispute over equipment was never known by others. The police found video equipment in Henry's car but not in Todd's apartment. The bigger mystery was how a once shining star could ever have fallen so far away from his role as America's Dad.

Chapter 7

The Unforgettable Tasha Dupree

The smoky haze inside a late 1960s Hollywood nightclub permeated the room wall-to-wall. The rolling roar of chatter, laughter and cocktail glasses clinking together provided the auditory backdrop from backstage. Peeking out from the corner of the curtain to get a glimpse of the crowd was a nervous young singer, Tasha Dupree.

Singing was in her blood. Still in college, she wanted to try to follow in her famous father's footsteps after his untimely death. Although she was only the opening act for a one hit wonder, it was Tasha's father's name that was drawing in a packed house for that evening.

Paying customers wanted to hear the comedy and bawdy hit song, "SugarTit" from the raspy voice of the one and only Dusty Savage. However, the crowd would first get their money's worth by hearing Nate Dupree's little girl belt out her own selections. Tasha wasn't planning on singing any of her father's hits. She didn't want the comparison but that was exactly what the crowd wanted to hear.

The band was playing a filler set as Dusty Savage arrived in the wings to wish Tasha well. While tugging at her trademark platinum blonde wig, Dusty said in her gravelly tone, "Break a leg, honey! If you do slip-up, just keep going. They're too drunk to notice." Tasha smiled in appreciation but her nerves had her fearing the worst.

The music faded as the emcee provided her first solo introduction, "Now, ladies and drunk men, we're going to start you off with Nate Dupree's pride and joy, his talented daughter Tasha. Please give a big welcome to the first solo performance of Miss Tasha Dupree." The crowd gave a thunderous applause as Tasha took a deep breath and hoped that her legs wouldn't buckle while headed onstage.

The music played and Tasha hummed her way into the lyrics of her first song. It was a catchy tune from long ago with a slight bounce to it but she was making it her own. The crowd seemed to be enjoying her renditions of old and new songs. They kept waiting to hear one of her father's unforgettable ditties that weren't on her playlist. Her set had ended and she felt the love. She gave thanks and started to exit when the crowd began to repeatedly chant, "Midnight Rose".

Tasha momentarily stood frozen. She looked off to the wings and saw Dusty standing there mouthing for her to, "Sing it!" The song, "Midnight Rose" was more than a familiar one for Tasha. It was her father's biggest hit. One that he had crooned many times including with her. Unrehearsed, unprepared and uncertain if the band even knew the song, she politely said, "It's been sung but thank you!"

The crowd's response became even more insistent as they stood in unison yelling for, "Midnight Rose". Tasha looked over to the band leader who smiled and gave the musicians his cue to begin playing. Tasha had never attempted this song on her own but she did her best to honor her father's memorable rendition. Her confidence rose by midpoint. At the end, the crowd gave her a standing ovation.

Tasha took her bows, waved to the crowd and gave Dusty a hug as she passed her in the wings. "Tasha Dupree, ladies and gentlemen." she could hear the emcee say as she hurried to her tiny dressing room. Sitting before her lighted mirror, she was reflecting upon more than her wilting make-up. She could see the reflection of her father looking back at her in resemblance of his face and in his song.

It was in that moment that Tasha's decision to not sing her father's songs changed slightly. Until she felt that she was a star in her own right, she'd close with "Midnight Rose". It would be her tribute to parental legacy. Afterall, what better way to end her act than to pay homage to the man who helped get her there? Audiences loved it.

Time passed and the music of the mid 1970s had changed with the ubiquitous onset of disco. Tasha enjoyed the dance rhythm that was a new genre. It was selling records and filling venues. Tasha had the first hit that she could call her own. It was a catchy tune that had a slight disco beat, topped the charts and gave her career a big boost.

Other songs from the same album followed her initial success and brought Tasha her first gold album. As if her sudden fame was not enough, her next two albums both went platinum. It had only been five years since Tasha began her career but she was now a bonified star in her own right. No more closing her act with Dad's old song.

The next few years brought more success with album after album followed by a heavy touring schedule. In the early years, Tasha enjoyed being on the road. She enjoyed seeing the world and being in a different city every night. After a while, what endeared her to the road in the beginning became her reason for tiring of it quickly.

She was in a different city every night, which meant a different hotel and different staff and a lack of permanency. It was empty and lonely and she missed her family and friends. Her tour entourage was a nice group of people but they were paid to be there. It wasn't the same as spending time with people who weren't on the payroll.

Their tour continued to the point that Tasha had difficulty recalling the city name of each evening's performance. She was becoming physically weak and struggled with lyrics including ones that she wrote. Well past the mid-point of the current tour, she was hearing jeers coming from the audience when she couldn't deliver her best.

Fatigue had taken over and despite her valiant efforts, Tasha was on the verge of collapse. She couldn't stand for the entire performance. Midway through her show, she'd have to sit in order to continue. It was becoming an artistic clash to see the singer sitting while dancers were dancing furiously around her. Audiences were disappointed.

The third consecutive year of touring was coming to an end and Tasha could barely continue on. Her schedule started early each day traveling to the next town, followed by sound checks, fittings, press and each day would end with a two-hour show. It was a grueling schedule and despite her youth, she couldn't keep up. Her body was breaking down and her spirit was already broken. At her last show of a long tour, she collapsed on stage. She was taken to the hospital where she was treated for exhaustion and dehydration.

As was the case for late 1970s touring acts, drugs and alcohol were a way of life. They were so prevalent that it would have been more conspicuous if drugs weren't offered than if they were. At first, Tasha wanted no part of it. She was a former choir singer with roots in gospel music. This drug scene was not her scene, at least not yet.

Adhering to doctor's orders for rest while simultaneously enduring the bemoaning of promoters for not being on tour, Tasha embraced her respite. She was doing her best to make time to enjoy a simpler life but her superstar status was working against her every effort.

She couldn't leave her house without being in disguise. Lunch out with friends had to be carefully orchestrated with bodyguards for her safety. After the murder of John Lennon, no super-celebrity was taking a chance with some lunatic seeking infamy as a legacy.

Knowing that her time off would be limited, Tasha felt the need for spiritual guidance. Her family had given to her a history of religious participation. As a result, Tasha decided to seek solace by visiting her former church. It had been a long absence and a long overdue return. Slipping in quietly one afternoon, she met with the minister.

During her absence from attendance, the previous minister had apparently retired and moved away. The reverend today was a much younger man. He was very handsome and since he wasn't a priest, it was a reasonable expectation that he might be married. Finding herself very attracted to this man, Tasha searched for a wedding band but his hand was free from indication of matrimony.

It was not a date or a husband that Tasha was seeking that day but it was the eventual result. After several months off from touring, she found herself in a whirlwind romance with the man she met while trying to find direction in her life. It became obvious that he was the direction that she was seeking when he decided to propose.

After an elaborate wedding and extended honeymoon, Tasha was feeling rested and ready to make her return to the stage. It was with her new husband's encouragement that she returned to the studio. Her talent resurfaced via a new album that debuted at the top of the charts. Her public was wanting a new tour and she felt ready to go.

With her husband by her side, Tasha took to the road with a more limited concert schedule than before. After six months of touring, Tasha's would be taking more time off to have her first child.

Settled in back at home, Tasha and her husband, Dex, became the proud parents of a baby boy. In honor of her late father, they named their son Nate. Everything was seemingly perfect for Tasha. She had a loving husband, a beautiful baby and a thriving career. It felt like her life was a dream come true but was to later become a nightmare.

After only four years of marriage and with a young son, life's way of keeping us humble came calling for Tasha. One day, she was at the studio working on her new album when she received a call. It was her nanny advising that her husband had collapsed and was taken to the hospital. Tasha hurried to be by his side but by the time she arrived, Dex had passed away. As Tasha stood in the hallway of the hospital in tears over her loss, a fan asked for her autograph.

Now a widow with a young child and a career still demanding her attention, Tasha threw herself into her work. She felt the need for adulation from her fans. She needed to feel loved and there was no better resource for immediate gratification than being onstage.

Her son was still her priority but she also had to support herself and her child. Her tour would have to continue with her son in-tow. It was a surreal upbringing for a child to be surrounded by thousands of people every night coming to see his mother. As Nate grew older, he came to accept that, despite Tasha's professing his priority, being a star would always come first. Stardom outshined her motherhood.

Before she knew it, Nate was finishing high school and on his way to college. His departure left his mother alone. She struggled with the reality that she was growing older as her career hit a slump. She could still draw a crowd but the venues were becoming smaller.

It had been several years since Dex died and busy with her son and her career, Tasha had never remarried. After loneliness set-in, she found herself attracted to her manager, Andy, who had always flirted. After years of dismissing his advances, Tasha decided to open the door to the possibility of them dating. The fact that they'd known each other for years gave the illusion they knew each other well. They married but the illusion was soon marred by drug use.

It didn't take long after being married for Tasha to see a noticeable change in her new husband. Andy went from being a kind soul to a demanding spouse. As both her husband and manager, he felt that it was now within his rights to make demands of her personally and professionally. He increased her tour schedule without asking her. He also had a cocaine habit that she previously knew nothing about.

Feeling as if she had married a stranger but not prepared to give-up on a new marriage, Tasha gave in more than she pushed back. It just seemed easier to give Andy what he wanted over arguing about not doing something. The hardest demand to succumb to was her tour schedule. It was even more grueling than her previous three-year tour that landed her in the hospital. She was soon worn out.

Andy insisted that if Tasha didn't tour, her career's slump that took her from playing stadiums to playing nightclubs would continue. She agreed with her husband that her career was sagging and she wanted it to thrive. She could only do so much physically and that's when Andy had her doctor begin to prescribe stimulant pills.

Tasha never was an artist who needed something to get her out of bed in the morning and again to sleep at night. That soon changed after only a few months of taking what she felt was safe since they were prescribed by her doctor. She had reached a point where she needed drugs to take the stage. Those drugs made her so high that she then needed drugs to bring her down after a show. After a two-year tour, Tasha was physically drained and it was starting to show.

Andy was singing the praises of Tasha's recent tour. Her record sales were at an all time high and so was she. When Tasha wasn't on tour, she was home tweaking out on drugs that she never really needed. She was restless and argumentative. She didn't sleep much and her weight had dropped dangerously low. She couldn't stop moving long enough to relax. Her voice was becoming a bit raspy.

Fearing the loss of Tasha's singing instrument, Andy pulled her out of the world of prescription drugs. Unfortunately, he took her with him into the world of cocaine as it could bring a more mellow high.

Tasha first protested the use of illegal drugs. She had previously looked the other way with Andy's use but that soon changed. After convincing her to "try it once", Andy soon had Tasha hooked on the highs and lows of cocaine addiction. Andy's cocaine use was always more of a recreational experience. Tasha began chasing the return of that first euphoric high but it could never quite be recaptured.

At her worst point, Tasha was performing at a large Las Vegas hotel that had caught on fire. Seeing the hallway filled with smoke and believing that she was trapped and going to die, Tasha chose to let cocaine alleviate her fear. Fire alarms blared while firefighters went door-to-door to save people. Tasha was shooting up when the door was broken down to save her. She was taken to a hospital for smoke inhalation. The doctor confronted Tasha on her needle track marks.

Hearing of his mother's close call on the news, Nate took the next flight to be by her side. They had always been very close and spoke on the phone frequently. However, Nate had not physically seen his mother in more than a year. Upon arrival, he was shocked at her condition. She had an alarmingly gaunt physique. Nate discussed with her doctor the cause of her condition. He was shocked to learn that his church-going mother was now a confirmed drug addict.

Enraged as to her condition, Nate confronted his mother on how this could have happened. Tasha was doing her best to downplay the severity of the situation but Nate was not buying it. He insisted on knowing who had led her in this direction but she stayed mum on the culprit. In the absence of facts, Nate could only assume that Andy was somehow involved. Afterall, he was with her and she had never displayed this kind of behavior until she married him.

Andy arrived at the hospital to take Tasha home so that she could rest before continuing her tour. Nate insisted that she be taken to a well-renowned drug rehabilitation facility in nearby California. As her husband, Andy had legal authority but Nate was about to play hardball. Nate had Andy arrested for drugs while his mother's attorney filed for Nate's power-of-attorney over her money and care. Tasha was sent to rehab while Andy was sent to stand trial.

The initial intake at the rehab facility provided for only occasional phone calls to advise loved ones that they were safe and doing well. Once progress was made, loved ones were permitted visitation, Nate made his way to meet with his mother. She looked tired but offered a big smile to her only child. They held each other in tears over Nate's concern for his mother and she for scaring her son.

As Tasha wiped away her tears, she looked at her son who had always been the strong image of his father, Tasha's first husband. Now, he had been reduced to a weeping protector of the woman who gave him life. "Mom, you know that you can't go back to living with Andy. You'll die!" Nate said to his mother's beleaguered face.

Tasha looked to her son for comfort. What she saw was the loving face of her first husband beckoning her. It was revisiting familiar comfort that she had not seen in a very long time. Tasha knew Andy was not good for her. She'd never again risk her life or her career. "I know, Nate. I have to figure out how to get him out of my life." she said in a defeated tone. "I'll take care of it!" Nate replied sweetly.

Together, Nate and Tasha enjoyed their visit until it was time for her to return to treatment. Nate hugged her tightly and said, "I love you, Mom. You're all I've got!" Tasha fought back tears as she said her farewell. Nate left to begin the arduous process of preparing for his mother's return by removing the legal claims of a dire spouse.

While Andy had his lawyers fighting to reduce his crime to a lesser charge and time served, Nate was combing through financial records. Nate closed all joint bank accounts that Andy was using to fund his defense. Without compensation, Andy's attorneys soon bailed on him leaving him with a public defender and time to serve.

Andy's conviction was the cause needed to have Tasha file for divorce, which she did. He demanded spousal support but Nate had managed to find some financial impropriety by Andy. He had fathered a child with another woman during his brief marriage to Tasha. He had been paying child support by forging her signature to checks. It was a crime that sent Andy away from Tasha forever.

Once Andy was removed from her life, Tasha began to flourish. She had a new lease on life with her son by her side. Her daily routine started with meditation and prayer followed by exercise and vocal practice. Her voice had suffered during her years of drug use but she managed to get it back to a range reasonably close to its prime.

As for her career, it had seen better days. Despite the fact that she rarely had a break from touring, her last hit record had been twenty years prior. The last few years of her touring had her singing the same old hits from years gone by and often lip-syncing to a track. The audiences dwindled in size. She needed new material to restart.

During her sabbatical to restore her health, Tasha began to work on a new album that was a departure from the others. It would be a collection of old standards that included her father's greatest hits. Her record label had their doubts about old styles being updated for a modern market. "Younger people won't be interested." they said.

In the end, the record company reluctantly agreed to give it a try and persistent doubts were soon proven wrong. Twenty years after her first hit, Tasha was back on top of the charts with new hits. The remix of old and new songs held an appeal that transcended age and genre. Tasha's father had posthumously saved her career.

At that time, hit songs always had a well-polished video. Tasha had the idea of recording her video using a technique that would allow her and her father to sing together. Using footage from some of his old televised performances, father and daughter took his song back into the halls of success. Tasha felt certain that he'd be very proud.

It was ironic that in the beginning of Tasha's career, she didn't want to ride on her father's coattails. However, when her career needed a boost, her father's songs, success and good name served her well. It brought a greater appreciation for his success and his struggles to achieve it. Tasha returned to touring to promote her new album. On tour, the crowd called out for her early hits. It reminded her of how the crowd called for her father's big hit "Midnight Rose" during her first performance with Dusty Savage cheering her on in the wings.

The effects of Tasha's years of drug use took a toll on her body. In her later years, she suffered from Hepatitis-C and eventually went into renal failure. The result was years of dialysis while she waited for a kidney donation. At one point, she took to publicizing her need for a kidney on a popular late-night talk show to seek help.

Tasha began a crusade to bring greater awareness to the need for organ donation, not just for herself but also for others. Her celebrity gave her a voice that she felt would be well-served by writing her autobiography, "Shouldering the Burden". It was a brutally honest account of how her charmed life as the daughter of a famous singer brought privilege but at a high price. Comparisons to his squeaky-clean image, at times, had her rebelling in song and in drug use.

Writing the details of her troubled marriage that drove her to drug addiction was like cleaning out a closet that was overflowing. The pain of professional setbacks was secondary to personal struggles. At the time of her book's inception, she thought it might be more of a cathartic effort. However, drudging up misery only brought pain.

Following in famous footsteps closed as many doors as it opened. It was hard for Tasha to be taken seriously as an artist when a father's legacy was her starting point. Once she managed to find success in her own right, the fight to stay at the top was ongoing and difficult. Adding to her struggles were the many people who always wanted something. She had to grieve the avarice and insincerity of others.

Tasha found herself too ashamed to share every detail in her book. At her lowest point, she had put drugs before her loved ones. In the spiraling existence of addiction, even the most loving person would sell their soul for a fix. It was hard for Tasha to admit to herself and others that she had fallen so hard. Emotions ran deep in confession.

In her final days, Tasha was surrounded by the love of her child and her family. It was the holiday season and she had to cancel her final performances due to illness. Her heart gave out and at the age of sixty-five, Tasha died with her son by her side. The world mourned the loss of her talent. Tasha Dupree would forever be unforgettable.

Chapter 8

Laugh Clown Laugh

"Come on, fat ass!" the group leader of a well-known boys' outdoor camping group yelled to a straggling, wheezing obese teen. The rest of the group refused to wait. Left behind were an impatient mentor and his struggling charge to return to camp before sunset brought night fall. Eddie endured yet another day's ridicule over his weight.

In the 1940s, Eddie Paulson was the chubby jokester that seemed to be part of every social group. His midwestern upbringing by his loving parents left him well-fed and it showed. He masked his pain with a self-deprecating brand of humor. It was easier to cope with the fat jokes when they came from his mouth and not from others.

By the time he was finishing high school, Eddie's hilarity had been fine tuned. It was to the point that people wanted his friendship just to enjoy his humor. He thrived on being the funny guy but once he was of college age, he had trimmed down and ruined his whole act.

His talent prevailed as he made his way off to college. Upon arrival, he majored in drama and theater. He studied side-by-side with fellow future thespians, some of whom became famous, including Eddie. Once his college years were behind him, Eddie was off to New York where, by talent and by luck, he landed on Broadway.

It didn't take long before Eddie's flamboyant persona, snarky style of humor and innate comedic timing caught the attention of others. He had dabbled in stand-up comedy. The audiences' responses were such that he soon had television offers. He pulled up stakes, headed to Hollywood and began his stardom one snark at a time.

Eddie found himself fielding offers from agents and studios after only one appearance on a late-night talk show. His natural gift for telling a joke and giving the proper pause for response had his star shining quickly. Cameos on various television shows and in films brought Eddie's fame quickly despite a slight effeminate demeanor.

Homophobia of the early 1960s had every gay entertainer staying deep in the closet. In Eddie's case, unless you were blind, deaf or in denial, there was no failing to recognize his obvious sexuality.

Despite his "bitchy queen" persona, Eddie was often cast in the role of a paternal setting. The reasoning might have been camouflage. If you stood a loving wife next to an obviously gay husband, perhaps nobody would notice but notice they did. In his own unintentional way, Eddie Paulson may have been an early pioneer for gay rights.

Audiences found him amusing enough to watch while ignoring a social stigma. Back in the 1960s, studios and actors never admitted that a star of any gender was gay. It would have been career suicide and anyone in the entertainment industry knew it. Eddie didn't care if people thought he was gay but he'd never put his career at risk. He did his best to dodge ongoing rumors of his so-called secret life.

Years rolled by and Eddie's career was thriving. He had more work and more money than he ever expected. When he wasn't spreading laughter, he was decorating his lavish, historic home. It was once the home of a major film star from Hollywood's early days. "Casa Eddie", as it was dubbed, was his sanctuary from a prying public.

Eddie surrounded himself with other celebrity friends. Some were co-stars and some were big stars. Together, they did what celebrities did back in those days to mingle; they drank and often heavily. It was not unusual for mid-day cocktail parties to spring up at the end of a busy filming schedule. Time and money being on their side, the Hollywood elite used these social settings as their opportunities to network for coveted roles. It became a situation of trust nobody.

All was fair in love and Hollywood and even the best of friends would stab each other in the back to land a lucrative deal. Perhaps it was a tv series or maybe a big budget film. It didn't matter. If one person wanted something, they'd stop at nothing to get it. Eddie was no threat to a leading romantic role. However, he could give stiff competition to any male seeking to land a leading comedic role.

It might be the show's father, neighbor or even eccentric uncle but if laughs were to be had, Eddie knew how to grab them. The result was that other actors seeking to further their careers felt the need to play dirty. Tabloid stories about Eddie's "secret life" had surfaced.

Stories about drunken house parties in all-male settings inferred the obvious despite the fact that the stories were all false. In the tabloid world, stories don't have to be true. They need only to be rumored. Most celebrities just brushed off the vicious and fictitious rumor mills of a less-than-reputable media but Eddie decided to fight back.

It was one thing if a publication implied that he was gay but to infer that he was having gay orgies was an absolute lie. Eddie sued and settled for a sizable amount with an agreement that his name would not be seen again in their rag. The sad fact was that these stories originated with a "friend" seeking to retaliate over losing a role.

What was true was that Eddie had become a functioning alcoholic and soon became known as a mean drunk. He now trusted nobody and alcohol removed what little social filter he once had. Once a few cocktails had been consumed, his insulting opinions were flung. His days as an invited guest to other celebrities' parties soon vanished.

Eddie once told one of his best friends that she'd never be a big star because she was "too fat" and then laughed about it. He also told another actress, whose mother was also an actress, that her mother reminded him of his dog because "they have the same whiskers." It was his escapades of inebriation that brought him replete animosity.

Eddie's gregarious nature was soon alone and lonely. His dog was not only his best friend but, at times, was Eddie's only friend. Eddie's drinking while in the company of fellow entertainers was bad enough. However, once alone at home, his drinking escalated to a dangerous point of blacking out. It had become a familiar sight for Eddie to wake-up on the floor with his dog whining to go out.

His life had become this shell of its former self. Previously, Eddie was hyper-organized, anxious to work and the consummate actor who knew his lines. Now, he'd show up onset reeking of alcohol, unshaven and unprepared for a full day's filming. Directors and producers were not amused. Word spread quickly among the studio executives that hiring Eddie, most likely, would lead to a production delay. Eventually, the roles grew fewer and fewer.

After a series of late studio arrivals holding up production over what was often a very small role, Eddie's phone stopped ringing. He did what alcoholics often do, which is to blame others for his misfortune when the blame was his own. Self-destruction prevailed.

Uncertain as to how to proceed but still undaunted, Eddie took to the club circuit. Afterall, he started by doing stand-up and he could always tell a good joke and work the crowd. Nightclubs were also the only setting where he could simultaneously drink and perform. He hit the ground running and was soon selling out small venues.

After his shows were over, Eddie usually had a few cocktails under his belt. Feeling no pain and with discretion set aside, Eddie often made his way to various gay bars. As he mingled with the same discretion as every other closeted gay man of that era, crowds soon gathered. Holding court for a gaggle of queens, Eddie played the jester and made them laugh. The pre-cellular lack of cameras left his attendance nothing more than a conversation piece for others to tell.

There were times when Eddie met a new "friend" for the evening. Despite diminished sobriety, Eddie always managed to refrain from public displays of affection with another man. His career may have been on a downward turn but Hollywood was such that his next opportunity might be just around the corner. He wasn't going to chance feeding the tabloids with the capture of an indiscrete photo.

There were men who intrigued Eddie enough to be invited back to his home more than once. It was rare but it did happen. There were even a couple of different extended relationships where the men wanted something more than a casual affair but Eddie shied away.

One man named Alfonso was an artist who spoke mostly Spanish and wasn't impressed by Eddie's celebrity. Eddie liked Alfonso but he wanted someone to be dazzled by his stardom. Another was a man named David who first seemed very much in love with Eddie. Eventually, David was more interested in money. During a trip to San Francisco, David threatened to derail Eddie's career. David fell out of a hotel window and died. Of course, it was ruled an accident.

Eventually, Eddie met a man named Liam who was studying to be a nurse. Despite a nearly twenty-year age difference, Liam and Eddie had an instant chemistry. Liam's presence had a positive effect on Eddie, in that, Liam encouraged him to quit drinking. It was not a well-received suggestion but it was a long-overdue one. If Eddie wanted to resurrect his good name, he'd have to quit what caused the downfall of what had once been a very successful career.

Eddie agreed to give sobriety a chance but it wouldn't be easy. In his mind, it was alcohol that took the edge off of his inhibition and allowed for his talent to shine. In reality, alcohol never brought his talent. His talent was innate and all he had to do was to let go of the self-loathing and doubts that haunted him early on as an obese teen.

Liam took Eddie to a twelve-step program to begin his recovery. Once there, Eddie expected everyone to be in awe of his celebrity status but nobody even mentioned it. Afterall, it was Hollywood. Celebrities in rehab were not an unfamiliar sight even in the 1960s. One of the twelve steps was to apologize for past indiscretions. Eddie had many on his list to accomplish this step so he got started.

He called on everyone. Family, former friends, co-stars, directors, producers and major studio bosses all got the same speech about forgiveness. For some, it was cathartic and for others it was met with indifference but that didn't matter. Eddie needed only to try and he did. One such studio boss gave him another chance and job.

This studio boss must have had a heart of gold as his falling out with Eddie was ugly and personal. Eddie had been insulting to this man's family, staff, cast and crew and yet, the man forgave him. It was inspiring. Eddie knew that he had Liam to thank for starting the ball rolling. Eddie let his guard down and for the first time ever, he felt true love for another person but still, it had to be discreet.

Lying together in bed one evening, Eddie and Liam enjoyed the afterglow of what two consenting adults do in bed together. It was a moment of romantic bonding that seemed unfamiliar to Eddie. Liam looked at Eddie and said, "I love you!" as Eddie smiled back.

The unrequited declaration made by Liam was not well-received. Eddie had never had anyone outside of a parent declare their love for him. He was sure of his feelings but was uncertain of how to respond. Liam's feelings were hurt by Eddie not declaring his love.

"Aren't you going to say anything back?" Liam asked. Eddie had an uneasy look upon his face and replied, "Do I really need to say it? You know how I feel about you." Liam's look of disappointment must have been obvious as Eddie felt regret. Together, they sat in silence momentarily as both tried to figure out what to say. "I love you, too!" Eddie said while looking awkwardly away as if Liam might take back his declaration of love. They smiled at each other as the evening ended with an embrace and a turning point as a couple.

Months passed and Liam had officially moved into Eddie's house. Eddie made is very clear that the 1970s entertainment industry was still intolerant of gays. It was expected and understood that they would be discreet in public while being openly gay to their friends. Together, they maintained a low profile and Eddie's sobriety.

Job offers were picking up for Eddie once he made amends with many of the powers that be at the studios. There were not a lot of film offers but television had always been where most of Eddie's opportunity originated. He continued to make appearances on a variety of different shows. However, the work wasn't consistent.

Eddie wanted either a show of his own or, at least, a steady role on a weekly series. After many discussions and considerable efforts by his agent, one opportunity came his way. He was offered a job as a regular celebrity on a game show. It was one that had been on the air for several years but was lagging in the ratings. The show's producers felt that Eddie's brand of humor would be a good match.

Uncertain of his longevity on this show, Eddie agreed to appear temporarily to test the waters. It didn't take long before his well-scripted one-liners were the hit of the show. Ratings shot up and so did Eddie's salary. Before he knew it, Eddie had been the star attraction for a few years. It was lucrative but creatively unfulfilling.

In the process of networking with other celebrities on the game show, Eddie met another closeted gay actor named Don. They soon became good friends and eventually, Don introduced Eddie to a man named Kirk who was a very handsome low-budget porn actor.

Eddie was fascinated by Kirk's genre as an actor and the two soon became friends. Liam was suspicious of Kirk and seemed jealous. Accusations of cheating were made by Liam to Eddie but were always denied. Liam felt that Eddie and Kirk could not be trusted when, in fact, they were just friends. Mistrust brought tensions.

As Eddie's friendship with Kirk grew, his relationship with Liam had suffered. They were arguing constantly. Every time Liam had to be gone from home, he felt that sexual escapades were being had at their home. Eddie soon grew tired of Liam's rants over what he saw as an innocent friendship. Liam wanted Kirk out of the picture.

While finishing his studies in nursing one day, Liam was lost in thought as to how he could encourage Eddie to repudiate Kirk. Not paying attention to his work, Liam suddenly heard the voice of the charge nurse, "Liam, NO! That syringe is empty. Pay attention or you could kill somebody. An empty syringe injection will cause a bubble in the patient's vein that could stop their heart." she said.

Liam regrouped and corrected his mistake but he thought a lethal injection without a trace of drugs seemed inviting. Eventually, he dismissed the idea of using such drastic measures on Kirk. Afterall, he wanted Kirk out of Eddie's life but he couldn't be a murderer, could he? Moving on to more reasonable ideas, Liam decided to give Eddie an ultimatum. Either end his friendship with Kirk or Liam would end their relationship. Liam felt Eddie would give-in.

Confident that love would prevail, Liam made his way home and waited for Eddie to return from the studio. Liam decided to do laundry and that's when he found what he believed to be proof of Eddie and Kirk's escapades. The laundry contained hand towels covered in dried semen and Liam knew it wasn't from him. Overlooking the possibility of Eddie's party of one, Liam was livid.

Eddie returned home at the end of the day expecting Liam to offer a warm reception but instead, a look of seething anger greeted him. Liam wasted no time in making his accusation and offering his proof. Eddie explained that he had partaken in an intimate moment prior to leaving for work but Liam refused to believe him. The two snarled at each other back and forth until the unexpected happened.

"Get the fuck out of my house!" Eddie yelled and continued, "I'm tired of you accusing me of something that I didn't do. If you don't trust me then you shouldn't be here." This was not part of Liam's vision for how the day would progress. After being together for years, he was shocked and hurt by Eddie's wanting him to leave.

"What am I supposed to think when you're running around with a porn actor?" Liam demanded to know. Eddie's temper began to boil over. He desperately wanted a drink but he would not allow false accusations to steal his sobriety. He also knew that alcohol would only make things worse. He opted not to drink but it was difficult.

"I don't care what you think anymore because no matter what the truth might be, you always think the worst. You don't trust me. If I wanted to be with Kirk or anybody else, I'd be with them. You think that I couldn't do better than you? Some male nurse?" Eddie yelled.

Liam was very hurt by what he felt was Eddie's bragging about being able to do better than him and by the insults to his profession. He stood there teary-eyed but refusing to give Eddie the satisfaction of an emotional breakdown. Liam did what so many of us are often guilty of doing, which is using words to hurt instead of heal.

"I may only be some lowly nurse but I don't have to hide who I am from the world. You're just some snickering clown for the world to laugh at five days a week on some silly game show. How does that make you better than me? I'll go get my clothes. I know you need the room in your closet." Liam said in a sarcastic tone. Liam left the room to pack his belongings hoping that Eddie would ask him to stay but he didn't. As he left the house quietly, Eddie gave Liam a silent stare on the way out. Once gone, Eddie broke down in tears.

Weeks passed and the reality of Liam's harsh words were seeming too true to ignore for Eddie. He was a snickering clown and it didn't matter if the world was laughing at him or with him. He was in a creative rut that allowed for no creative diversity. As long as he was stuck on the game show, he couldn't create new characters like he did on television shows or in films. His sole purpose had become the regurgitation of one-line zingers from writers he barely knew.

Seeking a new direction personally and professionally, Eddie made the difficult decision to leave the game show. He would be leaving a highly lucrative job without first knowing where he was headed. In the entertainment industry, very few people would forego a big paycheck without first securing something equally profitable.

As for his personal life, he hated to admit that Liam's claims of being closeted were accurate but they were also necessary. If Eddie was to ever openly have another man on display as his partner, it would have to be after he retired and didn't need to work. He was not yet ready to reveal his inner most secret to a public in denial.

His departure from the game show was behind him and his creative exploration was ahead of him. At that point, a public legal challenge presented itself in the form of a very bitter lover. Liam had hired an attorney to seek a substantial sum for either his years served as Eddie's spouse or for his silence. Eddie dug in and refused to pay. It amounted to nothing less than blackmail, which was illegal.

The press latched on to the story and Eddie dismissed it as nothing more than a disgruntled former assistant. Liam was outraged by the inference that he was anything less than Eddie's partner. The two went back and forth legally and publicly until both a winner and a loser were declared by the courts. Liam's case was dismissed due to a lack of evidence. Eddie felt vindicated while Liam remained bitter.

Adding to Liam's anxiety was that he had seen pictures of Eddie in the press with Kirk standing in the background. It felt like a very big "fuck you" from Eddie to Liam, who assumed they were now a couple. Liam hated the idea of some porn queen replacing him.

The reality of it all was that Eddie and Kirk really were just friends but that no longer mattered. What mattered now was that a bitter, jealous ex-lover was on the loose. Declaring a need for a better life, Liam suddenly left Los Angeles and was never heard from again. It was well after Liam's departure that a fateful day arrived for Eddie.

He was due at a studio for rehearsal early one morning and never showed-up. Producers called repeatedly but to no avail. Kirk had been listed as Eddie's emergency contact and so he made his way to Eddie's house. Unable to access the door without a key, he knocked and knocked but still no answer. Kirk then kicked-in a side door.

The security alarm bellowed its sonorous siren indicating that Eddie must have set the alarm last night. "Eddie, it's Kirk. Are you home? EDDIE, ARE YOU HOME?" he yelled in his best effort to be heard over the noise of the alarm. Kirk ran through the halls and up the stairs to the bedroom. "EDDIE, ANSWER ME!" kirk kept yelling.

He opened the door and there was Eddie sound asleep in bed. Kirk felt relieved to know he was just sleeping; except he wasn't asleep. Kirk walked around the bed and saw Eddie's face with eyes closed and a greenish blue skin color. At the age of fifty-five Eddie had died in his sleep. The cause of death was listed as a heart attack.

Weeks passed since the media surrounded Eddie's house after his death. Liam never returned for the funeral. Eddie's many celebrity friends mourned the loss of one of their own. The snickering clown had made them laugh for the last time. What wouldn't leave Eddie were persistent rumors that he may not have been alone that night.

Rumors ranged from a clandestine sexcapade gone wrong to a well-concealed murder. Eddie's many friends and fans refused to accept the coroner's ruling. There would be no intrigue over a simple heart attack. Eddie had the last laugh by leaving a mystery. He'd love it.

After the curious fans had subsided, a neighbor walked by Eddie's house with her son. "Look Mommy, a toy." the little boy said as he showed his find. The mother took it away. It was an empty syringe.

Chapter 9

The Curse of Bella Grace

Poetic instrumental notes of a finely skilled orchestra sang out to the packed audience in attendance of a beautiful and historic theater. The building's walls were covered in indescribable painted beauty while providing a perfect echo of melodic sounds for the dancers.

Swaying onstage like a free-flowing breeze was a talented and well-renowned ballet dancer, Bella Grace. In her earliest days before notoriety came calling, Bella was first known as Isabella Gray. Her birth name lacked the artistic flow befitting of a promising young dancer. She decided to give herself a more intriguing stage name. Bella being an obvious abbreviation of her birth name, Grace was decided upon because it seemed to match her innate dancing skills.

Prior to entering the world of professional dance and celebrity, Bella overcame a troubled start. The pains of scandal were followed by repeated tragedy but she managed to persevere and succeed. The struggles of her childhood began from her father's impropriety.

Charles Gray was a very successful San Francisco businessman and widower during the final years of the nineteenth century. Amassing a fortune by way of more than one industry, Charles became a publisher and financier. He sold his publishing interests to become a patron and connoisseur of the arts. He later married his second wife Mary, Bella's mother, who was an artist and the daughter of a working-class state politician. Charles and Mary soon had a family.

Bella was the youngest of four children. When she was barely past her toddler years, her father was involved in an elaborate financial scandal. It was alleged that Charles and several others knowingly participated in a scheme to bilk millions from investors. The result was financial ruin while barely eluding stiff criminal prosecution.

The scandal left her father in financial ruins and disgrace. Soon after, Bella's mother divorced her husband. Mary and her children were then forced into extreme poverty. As the years rolled on, Bella, her siblings and their beleaguered mother survived by teaching piano, dance lessons and art. It was a meager existence of hunger and uncertainty as to where they might all be sleeping each night.

It was through her mother's diverse artistic interests that Bella first became interested in dance in all forms. When money permitted, Bella took lessons in art, dance and theater. She excelled at every artistic effort. She was a natural, if not a bit of a phenom, in the field of dance. Her talent drew praise from her teachers and audiences.

Eventually, the family's situation improved by way of Bella's talent. While barely a teen, Bella left school, lied about being older and replied to a newspaper ad seeking dancers. It was for a touring dance company offering a small weekly salary doing ballet. Mary, being a parent of free-expression, consented to Bella's departure.

As fate would have it, Bella's dance company was headed to Los Angeles. What she wouldn't know upon departure was that her long-forgotten father, that she barely remembered, would make a brief reappearance. Bella's dance company was financed through the benevolence of an unnamed benefactor of the Los Angeles arts.

After weeks of rehearsal and a successful week of performances at the most prestigious theater in Los Angeles, the touring company would meet their benefactor. In a post-performance line-up while still in costume, the dancers, choreographer and director stood in formation as this very well-attired family greeted them one-by-one.

Intentionally positioned by the director to save the best for last, Bella waited her turn at the end of the line. She could see this man in a top hat and tails accompanied by a younger woman draped in furs and diamonds. Behind them followed a young girl of perhaps seven or eight donned in well-coiffed curls and an expensive dress.

Feeling hungry and tired, Bella waited impatiently for her turn at congratulations from this mystery man. Finally, the director came face-to-face with Bella as he introduced her to an older man with a charming smile. "And finally, Sir, we have our youngest star. This is Miss Bella Grace." the director said then continued, "Bella, please say hello to Mr. Charles Gray." Hearing his name, Bella fell silent. Could it be just a coincidence of name or could this be her father? "How do you do, Bella? You were superb." the man said sweetly.

Bella stood staring at the man uncertain of paternity as she had only seen a very old photograph of her father. Failing to respond to the gentleman, she was prodded by the director to give thanks, "Thank you, Sir! Nice to meet you." she said in a tone set by intimidation of the situation. He smiled as he stared curiously at her before leaving.

Days passed and the touring company only had one performance remaining before they disbanded and scattered their separate ways. Bella had no plans other than returning to San Francisco. She had to continue helping to make ends meet for herself and her family. It was not a preferred plan but, being so young, it was her only plan.

The evening of their final performance, the director came to her and asked that she go to the theater office. He declined to explain why but, following orders, she made her way through the halls to the office of the theater manager. Feeling as if she was in some sort of trouble, she knocked and waited. "Come in!" a man's voice said.

Bella opened the door and standing in the shadows of a slow sunset pouring through the shades stood Mr. Gray. He was alone and gave her a friendly smile before greeting her. "Bella, it's nice to see you again." he said. She failed to understand why she was there. "Thank you, Sir. It's nice to see you, too!" she replied politely to his smile.

Mr. Gray fidgeted nervously with his gloves as he seemed to be searching for words. Finally, he spoke. "Bella, the director tells me that you're from San Francisco?" he asked. Bella replied, "Yes, Sir. Is there a problem?" she replied in a soft tone hoping all was well. Mr. Gray walked closer to her but kept his distance. "No, Bella. There's no problem. At least, I hope there's no problem." he explained.

Bella seemed confused as to her presence and his or what it was that this man wanted from her. She remained silent as she waited for him to continue the conversation. He stepped closer to her and knelt down so that his towering height was not intimidating to her tiny stature. "Do I seem familiar to you?" he asked softly. Bella hesitated before continuing, "Your name is, Sir! It was my father's name." He smiled, leaned-in and said to her, "Bella, I think I am your father."

Bella's teary-eyed pool of emotion was the only response that she could offer. For as long as she could remember, he had always been a mysterious shadow in her life. Now, he was standing before her and seeming larger than life. He was real and she could see him and touch him. It was unexpected and seeming so very long overdue.

He reached over and touched her hand in a father's display of love. Her weeping brought him to the verge of the same as she threw her arms around his neck and embraced him with all of her strength. "Daddy!" she cried as he scooped her up and held her tightly.

Together, they held each other until her tears subsided and his were staved-off. "How did you know it was me?" she asked her father. He smiled and replied, "Because you look just like your mother and I assumed that 'Bella' was short for Isabella." She smiled and wiped her eyes as she was still taking in a very unexpected moment.

The evening was an end to one phase of Bella's life with the touring company but it was a beginning to her father being in her life. Her mother had always been very secretive about what had happened to her father. Her older siblings had told her of the financial scandal but she had always been too young to understand what that meant.

Before her departure to San Francisco, her father met with her and did something that he never had been able to do previously. He took his daughter for ice cream where they talked and laughed and discussed his past and her future. She had so many questions to fill in the gaps from a confusing overview from her older siblings.

He asked about his other children. Since they never had a kind word to share about him, Bella minimized her response. "They're well enough, under the circumstances." Her father asked about the family's financial situation. Bella wanted to be polite as not to ruin their reunion. "It's been difficult but we'll manage." She explained. Her father explained that after Mary divorced him and left, she refused to allow him to see his children. He moved to Los Angeles for a business opportunity. Once he had regained his finances, he wanted to help but, after many moves, they could not be found.

Her father explained that he was now working in the fairly new industry of motion pictures. Along with other investors, he owned a production company and a movie studio. He offered Bella a chance to work in films. They were silent pictures but Bella's talent as a dancer would work well in a visual medium. Knowing that her family was still relying on her income, she agreed to do films.

Bella would return to San Francisco to make the big announcement that she had located her father. Uncertain of how it would be received, she hoped that news of her working to support her family would be embraced. The day of departure, Bella's father escorted her to the train station as she promised to be back in a week to begin her new career in Hollywood. Bella was excited but still nervous.

As she was about to board the train, her father pressed some money in her hand. "Please, help your mother and the others. Please, tell them that they are always welcome to visit. I'll help them." he said with sincerity. Bella smiled, hugged him and boarded the train. She waved to her father as he waved back. Once the train departed, she counted the money and was a gasp at the thousand-dollar sum.

Upon arrival Back in San Francisco, she made her way to the dingy surroundings of her impoverished family. Her mother looked pale and thin as she often went without food if there was only enough to feed the children. Her siblings seemed anxious to greet her and hear of her adventure. "Tell us all about it." her mother said excitedly.

Bella did her best to describe her time in the touring company but that had become secondary to the bigger news about her father. After a detailed account of performances, Bella shared her big news with the others about the return of Charles Gray. Her siblings stared silently. Her mother sat with disinterest until Bella showed them his gift. She flashed her wad of cash as the others were sent wide-eyed.

After years of wondering where their next meal was coming from, Mary and her children would now be able to have a better life. Bella explained her offer to move to Los Angeles to work in films. Her family wished her well and after a few final days, Bella departed.

Bella arrived back in Los Angeles with her father waiting anxiously at the train station. What he had failed to mention to Bella was that his wife knew nothing of his second marriage to Bella's mother or of she and her siblings. Charles' wife, Ava, knew of his first wife's passing but due to the scandal, he felt that Ava would not marry him if she knew he had been divorced with four children.

Ava was from a very prim and proper aristocratic family from back east. Ava's family comes from "old money" and plenty of it. It was through Charles' marriage to Ava that he managed to regain his fortune. His father-in-law had invested heavily in Charles' financial ideas including the development of the largest movie studio in L.A.

Ava and Charles had a daughter, Ana, who was eight years old and through good breeding and a stern nanny she was well-mannered but lacking in parental bonding. Ava believed strongly that children were seen and not heard. Ana lived a privileged life of loneliness.

"Daddy!" Bella yelled as she hurried to hug her father. Her father offered a big smile and a warm embrace. "Bella, are you ready to get started with your film career? I have big plans for you." Charles said to his daughter. "Indeed! Just lead me to it." she replied.

Months passed and Bella had just completed her second film. Her first film was among the last of the silent films. It was a dance extravaganza that was modestly received by the critics. Her second film was an early "talkie" that allowed her to display her singing and dancing prowess. Still an unknown, her second film brought a rapid climb to fame and an instant demand for more films.

By the end of her second year in Hollywood, Bella was as big of a star as any back in those early days. She had money and prestige. She had offered to have her family live in Los Angeles but they chose to live off of her generosity while remaining in San Francisco.

While making a film, Bella learned that her father, his wife and their daughter had all perished in an infamous ocean liner sinking. Bella was devastated over her loss. It was the beginning of "the curse".

After the death of her father, Bella sought the comfort of a French actor named, Adam. It was a fast and tumultuous love affair that was on and off and frequently more off then on. As much as they loved each other, Bella's strong persona did not lend itself well to the yield of traditions dictated by their era. She was nobody's timid housewife. Her art was her passion and always first in her life.

Adam was frequently threatened by Bella's success. She was always the bigger star and it grated on his very French masculine pride. Still, they managed to spawn two children; Serge and Julia. Bella and Adam could agree on very little, except the love of their children. The only times of consistent peace and unity were when it came to attending to their children but their careers made demands.

In an effort to meet maternal needs in her absence, Bella had hired a nanny to attend to the children while she was in Hollywood. The nanny was a young, easily distracted girl who allowed the children to run freely with their mother's blessing. Outside of daily care, the nanny's purpose was keeping the children safe. She failed at her duties on a fateful day at the park causing a grim demise for both.

While parked near a pond where they stopped to feed ducks, the nanny failed to secure the brakes on Bella's expensive car. Nanny Joie was new to and unskilled at motor vehicle operation. When Serge and Julia wanted to pretend to be driving, Joie watched from a nearby bench. Suddenly, the motor started and the car jolted forward again and again until it ended up in the water. Joie was screaming for help as the children tried to escape but they drowned.

Bella had now lost her father, step-mother, half-sister and both of her children to misfortune. In the absence of Serge and Julia, Bella and Adam could not find comfort in each other and parted ways. Bella eventually met another man while performing ballet in Los Angeles. He was a troubled soul named Nigel. It was his dark mood of angst and anger that drew Bella closer to him. She believed she could heal his pain. The were together for two years and it was a time of extreme highs and lows. Nigel had been diagnosed with "circular insanity", which today is known as bipolar disorder.

Nigel's highs were moments of ecstatic serenity. Blissful and filled with laughter bringing joy to anyone within his company. However, Nigel's lows were excruciating depression that drew sorrow from the simplest of situations. Bella and Nigel's family never knew what they were walking into when they greeted him. Eventually, the uncertainty of life and pains of manic depression were too great.

On a sunny, summer afternoon Bella had press at the studio to promote her latest project. Nigel penned his farewell note in blood, locked himself in the attic of Bella's home and took his life by hanging. The death of another loved one in her life had become disturbingly routine. Bella could find it in herself to mourn Nigel's death but death had become her frequent visitor. It was as if she had to ask herself, "Who's next?", then wait for fate to come calling.

Despite her innate desire for love and attention, Bella found herself wanting to avoid romantic attachments from men in her life. It was seeming as if every time she loved a man, either he died or someone near him died. She didn't want to chance another fateful call from someone advising that another person's inevitability had arrived.

Seeking the company of females for comfort, Bella found the very comfort she needed in the form of a new friend and studio writer. Her name was Victoria but it seemed such a formal name that Bella dubbed her Vic. Brevity replacing formality seemed to bring a small comfort to a big star who was lost in grief. Vic's friendship gave Bella's life a new and unexpected direction to explore and define.

One beautiful fall afternoon, Bella had been working diligently on a new film that called for long and difficult choreography. It had been weeks of physically demanding dance requiring multiple takes. It was with Vic in the wings watching her every move that helped to get Bella through a grueling routine and demanding film schedule.

The end of the day arrived and sunset would soon befall them. Vic insisted they take a drive to have a bottle of wine and watch the earth's rotation bid adieu to a difficult day. As the sun grew smaller, the wine was had and a cold breeze demanded efforts to stay warm.

While listening to the radio in Bella's convertible, Vic dug in the back to retrieve a preplanned instrument of survival to a chilly fall evening. Unfolding a large, wool blanket, Vic took the fabric and tossed it over both of them. It would have been more effective to raise the top on the car and start the motor for heat. However, it would not have been as intimate. Vic smiled at Bella's wine filled laughter as the music set the mood. After several minutes of music and apprehension, Vic looked at Bella, leaned in and kissed her.

Uncertain as to why she did not recoil, Bella allowed herself to find Vic's soft lips sensuous and inviting. Never had Bella ever felt an attraction to another woman. Perhaps it was the feminine mystique that was absent from masculine companionship. The uncertainty of going with your emotions versus accommodating the lust of men. No matter the reason, Bella willingly allowed the kiss to linger. She liked it and she wanted to do it again and again. Vic was her muse.

It didn't take long after their sunset ride that they found purpose in their journey. After only a few weeks of private affections and secret rendezvous, Bella and Vic were declaring their intentions toward each other. It was much to Bella's surprise when the day arrived that, without the influence of alcohol, she declared her love for another woman. Vic returned Bella's affections in a tearful reply.

Despite the social stigma and puritanical mores of the era that was the early twentieth century, these two ladies became more than just friends. As an artist, Bella felt no need to hide her love for another person of such strong caliber as Victoria. However, as a movie star, she had to make her choice to either sacrifice her career or accept what so many others were doing, which was live with a big secret.

Unwilling to give up a career that she had worked for years to achieve, Bella opted for quiet splendor over a boisterous scandal. It wasn't ideal but it was propitious. She and Vic could be as open as they wanted to be behind closed doors but once they opened, it was discretion that set the tone. In the confines of their era, they both accepted the inevitable and held their tongues to the public as they spoke freely to friends and other artists. Bella felt it was a new life.

After mourning the loss of her family, her lover and her children, she had found love in a very unexpected way. Unconventional as it may have been, it felt as if she was in love for the first time. It felt as if her grief was a bad dream that was long-since over. It felt as if she and Victoria would be happy forever. Love prevailed over sorrow.

After years of dodging the press over her personal life, Bella took the advice of a French friend and decided to relocate to France. She had heard of and observed the "vivire et laisser vivre" (live and let live) attitudes of the French. It was time to permit her true love for another person to be more overt than was permitted in America.

Together, Bella and Vic gathered their pride and their belongings and moved to the French city of Nice. Bella was still a viable star in Europe and if America no longer wanted her, another audience would embrace her. As an artist, Bella felt that she had been forcing herself to compromise her ideals and it stifled her creativity. Now, she was as open as she dared to be and nobody even batted an eye.

Making every effort to immerse themselves into a new culture, this daring duo took lessons to learn the language. They studied French architecture and art. They even learned to cook French food. It was the most urbane existence that anyone could possibly accomplish. Time brought them love of life and it was a seemingly perfect life.

Unfortunately, perfection is often accompanied by interruption. It came in the form of a very bizarre accident that was unlikely to be conceived by any reasonable expectations. One evening, Bella and Vic were on their way to a hotel to meet a friend for cocktails. On her way out, Vic suggested that Bella wear a wrap due to the cold night air. Bella, attempting French attire, insisted on a long scarf. Vic protested stating that the scarf offered no relief from the cold.

"Je vais a la gloire" (I'm off to glory) Bella said in dramatic irony. She climbed into her convertible with Vic manning the wheel and they sped away. Almost instantly, the scarf became entangled in the axel. Suddenly, the scarf knotted around Bella's neck and she was yanked from the car and thrown to the ground nearly decapitated.

It was a dramatically tragic end to a life that vacillated between blessed and cursed. After humble beginnings, fame and fortune had brought her the blessings of success. Once success became familiar, the cruelty of fate seemed to be forever just around the corner. Bella previously said to the cast of her life's performance, "When my time comes, please don't mourn my loss; celebrate my time with you."

Victoria was devastated over the departure of her beloved Bella. It was a two-fold tragedy for Vic. Not only did Bella meet her maker in the most gruesome of manner but their time together was to be honored by only a trusted few. While the rest of the world spoke freely of their love for Bella, Vic could only do so as a fan of her work. Otherwise, Vic would besmirch Bella's posthumous image.

Given the fact that financial assets were held only in Bella's name, Vic was forced to leave France without an inheritance. Everything was under French law and legal bestowment to family in America years prior. Vic had to return to her career as a Hollywood writer. She gathered what was hers and boarded an ocean liner to America.

While onboard the ship, Vic found herself in a pensive state late one evening while strolling an aft deck. It was a quiet moment of grief and reflection in a spot that seemed abandoned by slumber of the other passengers. The sky was clear and well-lit by the moon that also set a mood that was seemingly more for lovers than mourners.

Vic stood there chilly in the dark of night with an ocean breeze that surrounded her. Ironically, the only garment to help stave off the cold was one of Bella's scarves around her neck. As she watched the wake of the churning waters left behind by the massive propellers, it felt as if she was watching Bella making a final drift from her life.

Vic took the scarf and threw it into the breeze to bid farewell but a sudden gust drove it onto a flagpole just below the bridge. It was teasing Vic's need for it to be in the water. Carefully leaning over the rail, she tried to free the scarf. Her reach was too short so she climbed one rail higher. The wind prevailed. Over she fell into the water and reunited with her love by call of the curse of Bella Grace.

About the Author

JT DeBold
Father and Son

JT DeBold is a full-time father and dedicated humanitarian enjoying a peaceful existence in the Blue Ridge mountains. His other literary efforts include, *"Life Times Nine"*, *"The Guest House Chronicles"*, *"Eight Found Queens"*, *"The Pink Reich"*, *"The Transient Realm"*

Author contact: JTDeBold@gmail.com

CPSIA information can be obtained
at www.ICGtesting.com
Printed in the USA
BVHW030904100720
583428BV00001B/68